"He's taunting you, Grace. You need to stop this right now."

She shook her head. "This guy knows something, Alex. He has to be the killer."

"This is getting out of hand. First he gives you an anonymous call, then he sends you a puzzle to find his hidden message, and when you do, there's another clue that threatens you. This guy is setting you up for something bad, and I don't like it. This is a matter for the police."

She glared at him. "I've been trained to follow a story wherever it goes. I'll keep working on this whether you help me or not."

"Grace, I don't want to see you get hurt."

"I'm not going to get hurt. And I'm not giving up," she said and then stormed off.

She was determined to follow through on this, and Alex knew he'd do what he'd done ever since they were children. He'd be right there with her, looking out for her. How could she still have a hold on him after all these years and after all they'd gone through? Maybe if he helped her with this case he could finally close the chapter on Grace Kincaid and put her out of his life permanently.

Books by Sandra Robbins

Love Inspired Suspense

Final Warning
Mountain Peril
Yuletide Defender
Dangerous Reunion
Shattered Identity
Fatal Disclosure
*Dangerous Waters
*Yuletide Jeopardy

*The Cold Case Files

SANDRA ROBBINS,

former teacher and principal in the Tennessee public schools, is an award-winning multipublished author of Christian fiction who lives in the small college town where she grew up. Without the help of her wonderful husband, four children and five grandchildren who've supported her dreams for many years, it would be impossible to write. As a child, Sandra accepted Jesus as her Savior and has depended on Him to guide her throughout her life. Her writing ministry grew out of the need for hope she saw in the lives of those around her.

It is her prayer that God will use her words to plant seeds of hope in the lives of her readers so they may come to know the peace she draws from her life verse, *Isaiah* 40:31—"But those who hope in the Lord will renew their strength. They will soar on wings like eagles, they will run and not grow weary, they will walk and not be faint."

YULETIDE JEOPARDY

SANDRA ROBBINS

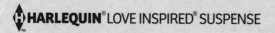

Recycling programs
for this product may
not exist in your area.

LOVE INSPIRED BOOKS

ISBN-13: 978-0-373-67587-6

YULETIDE JEOPARDY

Printed in U.S.A.

Let all bitterness, and wrath, and anger,
and clamour, and evil speaking,
be put away from you, with all malice:
And be ye kind one to another, tenderhearted,
forgiving one another, even as God for Christ's sake
hath forgiven you.
—*Ephesians* 4:31–32

To Kathy

A Great Friend and Critique Partner

ONE

The WKIZ-TV van skidded to a stop near the police cars blocking the entrance to the Memphis-Arkansas Bridge, and Grace Kincaid jumped from the vehicle before her cameraman had time to turn off the engine. The blue lights on the cruisers flashed in the cold December morning fog that drifted up from the Mississippi River below.

She held up her identification badge, which hung from a lanyard around her neck as she ran toward the officers who stood beside the cars. "Grace Kincaid, WKIZ. I had an urgent message that a man who's threatening to jump from the bridge wants to talk to me."

Captain Wilson, who she had interviewed once, pointed toward the middle of the bridge. "His name is Timothy Mitchell. Do you know him?"

Grace's eyes widened, and she nodded. "His son was a friend of mine in high school. He committed suicide on this bridge when we were seniors."

"We found that out," he said.

Grace's mind raced at the possibilities of this story. The father of her high school boyfriend was threatening suicide on the same bridge where his son had died, and he'd asked for her. Stories like this came along maybe once in a career. If she handled this right, the video would make a good addition to her application when she decided to apply to the networks again. She had to handle this carefully if she was to have a happy ending to this story by getting Mr. Mitchell safely off the bridge.

She turned to Captain Wilson. "Has he asked for anything else?"

"Mr. Mitchell asked for you and Detective Alex Crowne, but he's not here yet. You can wait here until he arrives," Captain Wilson said.

Grace groaned inwardly. Just what she needed. This story had just gotten a lot more complicated. She hadn't seen Alex since the wedding of their best friends Laura Webber and Brad Austin six months ago, and he'd ignored her then. He would probably do the same thing when he arrived at the bridge because he still couldn't stand to be near her. Instead of accepting his part in their failed romance, he had chosen to blame her, and she supposed he always would.

Grace shook her head. No way was he going to ignore her today and let this story slip through her fingers. She didn't need Alex Crowne to help her with a man she'd known well once upon a time. With any luck she could have Mr. Mitchell down and be gone before Alex arrived.

"No, thanks. He can join me when he gets here." A cold gust of wind whipped her coat around her knees, and she shivered at the early-morning chill. She pulled her gloves from her coat pocket, tugged them on and nodded to her cameraman Derek. "Let's go. Be sure you keep that camera on. This will be our lead-in story on the noon and six o'clock news."

Derek nodded. "Gotcha."

Grace hurried toward the two officers who stood up ahead in the roadway next to the knee-high concrete barrier that separated it from the pedestrian walkway. As she came closer, her heart sank at the sight of the man who straddled the walkway railing on the river side of the bridge. His eyes were closed, and he swayed back and forth on the handrail as his long, white hair blew about his face.

The years had taken a toll on the once-handsome man. She'd heard that after his son's death he had spiraled into a deep depression and had spent time in and out of mental institutions. Tears filled Grace's eyes. The man balancing on the railing just feet away from her looked nothing like the wealthy businessman she'd once known.

One of the officers glanced from her to Mr. Mitchell as she approached. "Just let him talk and tell you what's on his mind. Maybe you can distract him long enough for us to get him off that railing."

Grace glanced around to make sure Derek had the camera rolling and nodded. "I'll try."

She cleared her throat. "Mr. Mitchell," she called out.

Another gust of wind blew across the bridge, and the man wobbled as he struggled to maintain his balance. For a moment it looked as if he might fall to the river below, but he steadied himself. "Is that you, Grace?"

Chills rippled up her spine at the sight of the gaunt figure perched on the railing. She took a deep breath and stepped closer. "Yes. I understand you wanted to see me. What can I do to help you?"

The man didn't speak for a moment. His eyes narrowed, and his gaze raked Grace. Her skin burned as his intense stare bored into her very soul. "You can find out who murdered my son."

Grace didn't know if it was the force of Mr. Mitchell's words or the veins that stood out in his neck and face that frightened her the most. "Mr. Mitchell, Landon committed suicide. Don't you remember? His car was found parked on this bridge. The door was open, and the keys were still in the ignition. There was a note on the seat that said he was sorry."

His eyes blazed with fury. "He didn't commit suicide. The note was printed off a computer. Landon hated typing on the computer. He would have left a handwritten note. Everybody was too quick to decide it was suicide."

She shook her head and frowned. "Mr. Mitchell, I noticed changes in Landon during the two years before he died. He started skipping school, his grades dropped and he cut himself off from his old friends. I thought he was going through some kind of depression, so I wasn't surprised when he killed himself."

The man closed his eyes and yelled at the top of his voice. "He didn't kill himself! He was murdered. It was that secret group he joined that killed him. You knew about it and didn't tell anybody."

Grace's eyes grew wide, and she held up her

hand. "Mr. Mitchell, please be careful. You're going to fall."

The words were no sooner out of her mouth than another wind gust whipped across the bridge. The loose-fitting, unbuttoned coat he wore flapped around his body. He grabbed the bar he straddled and clamped his legs around the base of the railing as he wobbled from side to side. Grace drew in a sharp breath and released it when he steadied himself.

She waited until he'd regained his balance before she spoke. "I understand how hard his death must have been for you. I wish I could have done something to help him, but he shut me out of his life. He never told me he joined a secret group. What makes you think he did?"

"Because after his death I found money hidden everywhere in his room. And I also found his journal. It was filled with all kinds of rambling entries about his successful deals and how much money he and his partners had made. There was a wolf's head drawn on every page."

"I never heard him say anything about wolves. Maybe it was just his way of doodling on the page."

Mr. Mitchell shook his head. "No, it was more than that. One night I went into his room when he was sleeping to cover him with an extra blanket, and I saw a wolf's head tattooed on his shoulder. So don't tell me there wasn't a secret group. I know there was. They were evil, and they killed my son." The last words ended in a sob.

"If you're right about this, I would like to help prove it. You say there was a journal that told about this group. Where is it now?"

He reached in his coat pocket and pulled out a leather book. "Here it is. I've read it over and over ever since he died."

"Would you let me look at it?" Grace inched forward and stepped over the low barrier onto the pedestrian walkway.

"Grace, stop right there. Don't get too close." Her heart thudded at the voice that came from behind her. It didn't matter how long it had been since she'd heard it. She'd know it anywhere. Alex Crowne had arrived on the bridge, and his command reminded her of the tone he'd used when cautioning her about something when they were children.

She frowned and shook her head. They weren't children anymore, and he'd long ago given up the right to be concerned about her safety. She arched an eyebrow and glanced over her shoulder. "It's all right, Alex. I just want to see the journal."

Mr. Mitchell tilted his head back and laughed before he glared at Alex. "So Detective Crowne who supposedly solves cold cases came, too." He leaned forward. "When I read in the paper you had been picked to help head up the new Cold Case Unit with the police, I begged you to solve my son's murder. When are you going to do it?"

"I looked into the case like I said I would do," Alex said, "and I told you I wasn't able to find any new evidence that his death was anything but a suicide."

Grace inched closer. "Mr. Mitchell, I'm sure Alex will be glad to look into Landon's death again." She turned her head and glanced at Alex over her shoulder. "You'll do that, won't you?"

Alex looked at her, then to Mr. Mitchell. "Of course I will."

Grace smiled and turned her gaze back to Landon's father. "We'll both see what we can find out. Now why don't you give me the journal and come down from the railing?"

Alex stepped over the barrier and came to a stop behind her. "No, Grace. Don't get any closer."

Without looking around, she waved Alex off. "It's okay." She moved closer to the railing and stretched out her hand. "I'm a reporter. If I see anything that makes me think Landon was murdered, I'll find out who did it."

Mr. Mitchell started to hold out the book but pulled it back. "Do you promise you'll find out who killed him?"

"I promise I'll look into his death, and Alex said he would also."

Hesitantly, he sat up straight and held out the book. Another strong gust of wind swept across the bridge, but it wasn't the sudden breeze that chilled Grace. Her skin prickled at the change in Mr. Mitchell's face. Whereas moments ago he had looked like a grieving father, his eyes now held a maniacal glare, and he stared at her as if seeing her for the first time.

"Grace, be careful!" Alex's warning came too late.

Grace reached out to take the journal. Before she could touch it, Landon's father hurled the book into the air and grabbed her by the wrist. "You can look at it with me at the bottom of the river."

Grace slammed against the bridge railing and gaped in horror as the book sailed downward toward the river. She looked up into Mr. Mitchell's crazed eyes and tried to break free, but it was no use. He held her in a viselike grip. "You know who killed my son."

"Grace!" Alex's panicked yell reached her, and she struggled to twist free.

Mr. Mitchell's hold on her tightened, and with a loud scream he fell backward off the railing but managed to clamp his free hand around the handrail. With one hand circling her wrist and the other clutching the railing, he dangled in midair and pulled her toward him.

Grace clawed for a hold on the railing with her free hand and watched in horror as he uncurled one finger from his grip on the handrail. He grinned and lifted another finger. Her feet lifted from the walkway, and she screamed at the excruciating pain radiating up her arm. She tried to wedge her feet between the metal rods that supported the railing, but she couldn't grab a foothold as his weight pulled her closer and closer to the top of the railing. In a few seconds she would be pulled from the bridge to a watery grave below.

Just when she thought all hope was lost, Alex's left arm encircled her waist, and he stretched his right one over the railing in an effort to reach Mr. Mitchell. The two uniformed officers appeared on either side of her to help Alex. Before they could catch hold of Mr. Mitchell, he released his hold on Grace's wrist and the railing, but Alex grabbed him by the sleeve of his open coat before he could fall.

"Help me pull him up," Alex yelled as he tightened his grip on Mr. Mitchell's coat. The officers reached down to assist.

Before they could pull him to safety, Mr. Mitchell threw back his head, released a bone-chilling laugh, and wriggled out of the coat. Grace had a split-second glance of the surprised look that flashed across his face before he plummeted toward the murky waters below. With them free of Mr. Mitchell's weight, she and Alex tumbled backward and landed on the walkway pavement with his arms wrapped around her.

She only had a moment to realize she was safe before Alex was on his feet and rushing back to the railing. She sat up and watched him lean over the railing and scan the river below. He turned to the officer next to him. "I don't see him. Notify harbor patrol where he went into the water. If we're lucky, we may be able to recover his body before the current carries it downstream."

Alex's shoulders sagged as he continued to look down at the water. After a moment, he turned and glared at her. Grace tried to rise, but her shaking legs wouldn't cooperate. Alex strode back to her, grabbed her uninjured arm and lifted her to stand next to him. She pushed a lock of hair out of her face and struggled to keep from bursting into tears. "Thank you, Alex. If it wasn't for you, I'd be dead right now."

The muscle in his jaw twitched, and his eyebrows drew down across his nose. He released a long breath and shook his head. "I've seen you do a lot of crazy things, but nothing can top what you did today."

She started to answer, but she noticed Derek still held the camera. "Derek, you can stop now. Go on back to the van and wait for me."

He lowered the camera and glanced from her to Alex. "Are you sure you're all right?"

"I'm fine. I'll be with you in a few minutes." Her wrist throbbed, and she massaged it as she watched Derek walk away. Then she turned back to Alex. Anger boiled up in her, and she took a step closer to Alex and stared up into his angry eyes. "May I ask what your problem is, Detective Crowne?" she hissed.

He didn't back away from her. Instead, he leaned toward her until they were face-to-face. "My problem? It was your problem. You almost got yourself killed. Why didn't you wait for me to get here? I might have been able to talk him down off that railing."

Grace straightened her back and stared at him.

"I had no idea when you'd get here, and I wanted to get Mr. Mitchell down as quickly as possible."

"And you wanted to be the main rescuer in the story, didn't you? You forget I know you too well, Grace. Your story on the noon news would sure look a lot better if you'd saved a man from a watery grave without the help of the police."

Her face grew warm, and she shook her head. "I think he was determined to end his life no matter who was here."

"Maybe," Alex said. "But we might have avoided the attempt on your life. I told you not to go any closer, and you didn't pay any attention to me. That shouldn't surprise me since you've never listened to me about anything."

His words cut deep, and she struggled to keep from bursting into tears. "What do you mean? Have you forgotten I'm the girl who followed you everywhere from the time we were ten years old? And that I'm also the girl who loved you and you threw my love away as if it was nothing? I'd say you're the one who never listened."

He shook his head and gave a sarcastic chuckle. "I guess it's true. Two people can see a situation and interpret it in an entirely different way. If I remember correctly, it was you who walked away from me without caring how I felt."

She took a step back from Alex and tried to

stem the tears welling in her eyes. She'd never been able to make him understand her side of their breakup, and she probably never would. It saddened her to think their once close friendship had come to this.

She lifted her chin and took a deep breath. "Who are you to talk about caring? You haven't even asked me how I'm feeling after almost taking a hundred-foot dive into the river. For your information I didn't ask to come here today, and I sure didn't ask to almost get killed. I was trying to save a man's life." Her battle to stop her tears failed, and she wiped at one that slipped down her cheek. "It turns out I didn't help, and your attitude has turned a bad day into an even worse one. I'd like to say it was nice seeing you again, but it wasn't."

Alex raked his fingers through his hair. "Grace, don't you understand—"

She held up her hand. "I think you've made your feelings very clear, Alex. Now I need to get back to work."

Clutching her fists at her side, she whirled and stormed down the walkway in the direction of the station's van. She'd failed to get the story of stopping a man from committing suicide that she'd first visualized when she set foot on the bridge. Instead of a piece to add to her résumé, she'd ended up with the last tragic moments of a man's life.

She didn't think she would ever forget the look on Mr. Mitchell's face right before he plunged to the river. She needed to get back to the station and decide how she would use the footage on the noon newscast, but at the moment she couldn't bear to think about the sad events on the bridge this morning. Maybe when she had calmed down, she could reflect on all that happened on the bridge today, but right now she needed to get as far away from it as possible.

Alex watched Grace stride away from him. Her blond hair glistened in the sunlight that had chased off the early-morning fog. She held her back erect, and anger oozed from every pore in her body. That was his doing. He should never have attacked her like that. After all she'd just had the scare of a lifetime, and he hadn't helped any with his harsh words.

He'd spoken before he had time to think. But he'd been so scared when he saw Mitchell grab her arm and go over the side of the bridge. At first he couldn't move, and then instinct kicked in. He had his arm around her and was pulling her backward before he realized what was happening.

He raised a shaking hand and brushed it across

his eyes. Regret that he hadn't been able to save Timothy Mitchell hit him like a kick in the stomach, and he knew it would be a long time before he could forget the look on the man's face when he'd truly realized at that last moment he was about to die. But he had to keep reminding himself Grace had lived. If he'd been a second later, she would be at the bottom of the Mississippi River with Mr. Mitchell right now. He almost groaned aloud at the thought. As usual, their meeting today had ended like many others in the past, but this one was his fault.

His eyes followed Grace, who had stopped to talk with Captain Wilson, and he wished he could take back the harsh words he'd spoken earlier. He couldn't, though, just like he couldn't undo the past.

He'd had many tense moments since he'd joined the force, but today had to be the worst he'd ever experienced. At the moment he'd thought she was going over the bridge, he didn't think of her as the woman who had broken his heart. He remembered her as the little girl who had shared his childhood with him. He had to make her understand how scared he'd been.

Alex turned to the officers who'd gathered at the railing and now watched the rolling water. "Do you need me for anything else?"

One of the officers who had tried to reach Mitchell shook his head. "There's not much more to do here. Thanks for the help."

Grace turned away from Captain Wilson and headed toward her van. Alex took a deep breath and jogged to catch up with her. She'd opened the door and was about to climb into the van when he called out to her. "Grace, wait. I want to talk with you."

She closed the van's door and glared at him as he approached. Her eyes flashed with anger when he stopped in front of her. "Do you want to berate me further for my bad judgment?"

Alex swallowed. "No. I wanted to make sure you're all right and apologize for the way I spoke to you on the bridge. You'd just seen a man die, and you were almost killed yourself. After all you became a victim, too, when Mitchell tried to kill you. I shouldn't have spoken to you the way I did. I'm sorry."

She frowned and shook her head. "So after all these years, your only concern for my welfare is because you saw me as a victim on that bridge."

He gritted his teeth and leaned closer. "You know that's not true, Grace."

"You still hate me, don't you?" She tilted her head to one side. "It's sad to think that after all these years we find it difficult to be around each other."

He took a deep breath. "Yeah, but every time we're together, it ends with angry words like it did on the bridge this morning. I don't want it to end that way this time."

She looked at him for a moment before she spoke. "Neither do I. I'm always sad afterward when that happens."

He sighed. "Me, too, but it doesn't change anything. There's too much history between us, Grace."

She opened her mouth to speak but didn't say anything. After a moment her shoulders sagged, and she nodded. "There is, and there's no way to undo the past. All we can do is try to make the best of it. I'd like for us to at least be civil when we run into each other, though."

"I hope we can in time," he said.

"Maybe we'll have time to make it happen while we're trying to find out the truth about Landon's death."

For a moment he thought he'd misunderstood her, but the determined look in her eye told him she knew exactly what she had said. "You can't be serious."

"Oh, but I am." She glanced around as if checking to see if anyone could overhear them before she lowered her voice. "What if his father was right and he was murdered?"

Alex shook his head. "Just because Mr. Mitchell says so doesn't make it true. The police did a thorough investigation, and they believed it was suicide."

"But still…"

"Suicide, Grace. That's all there is to it."

She arched an eyebrow. "So are you saying you won't help me find out the truth? We both promised him we would find out about Landon's death."

Alex stepped closer and frowned. "That was before the man tried to kill you. I think that canceled all promises."

"No, it doesn't. What if he was right and Landon was murdered? Did you ever hear anybody talk about a secret society at school?"

Alex thought for a moment before he responded. "I suppose I did. There was always talk about some mysterious group who lurked in the shadows. But I thought it was just gossip."

"What if it wasn't? What if there was a secret group and they killed Landon?"

Alex glanced at his watch. "I don't have time for this, Grace. I have real unsolved crimes I'm working on. Landon's death was a suicide. I have better things to do than go chasing after some silly rumor that circulated in our high school twelve years ago."

He started to turn away, but she grabbed his arm. "No, I'm not going to let you ignore this. We made a promise to a man right before he died. We may find it hard to be around each other, but that doesn't release us from doing what is right. We have to find out the truth, Alex."

He stared at her a moment before he pulled loose from her grip. "Although Landon's body was recovered, the medical examiner couldn't establish for certain the cause of death. So the case was never officially closed. Since it's a cold case, I'll look into it again. If I find out anything, I'll let you know."

She shook her head. "If it's a cold case, you have a responsibility to investigate it. And I have an obligation to my station. I'm not about to let this story go."

Understanding dawned, and he chuckled. "Oh, I get it. All your talk about doing what's right was just a ploy to get me to help you with a big story. What do you want, Grace? Are you tired of being back in Memphis and you need something that can get you back to the major networks?"

Her face flushed, and she shook her head. "No, Alex. I want the truth, and I'm not going to give up until I find it. I worked as an investigative reporter before I went to the anchor desk, and I can do it again. It would help to have the police involved with this, too. But if you don't help me, I'll just have to do it on my own."

"You're still as headstrong as ever." He studied her for a moment. "I don't believe you want the truth, but it so happens I do. You're right about one thing. It is my job to work a cold case, so I'll help you investigate Landon's death."

She swallowed. "How can you work with me on an investigation if you hate me so much?"

His shoulders sagged, and he shook his head. "I don't hate you, Grace. I don't trust you."

Tears sparkled in her eyes, but he didn't blink. He'd seen enough of her tears through the years to know it was her way of getting what she wanted. He cleared his throat and glanced down at her arm. "I need to get back to work, and you need to go to a hospital and get that arm checked."

She nodded. "Derek is going to take me by the hospital before we go back to the station." She started to climb in the van but turned back to face Alex. "You're right about a lot of things about me, Alex. I made some mistakes in the past, but you did, too. And you're wrong about my reasons for wanting to find out the truth about Landon's death. I hope you can come to see that."

He didn't know how to answer her, so he shook his head and stepped back from the van. He watched it drive away before he walked to where he'd parked his car.

When he'd gotten out of bed this morning, he'd expected a routine day at work. So far there had been nothing routine about it. He'd seen a man fall to his death, and he'd prevented Grace from following him into the Mississippi River. Now he was about to take another look at a cold case that hadn't produced a lead in twelve years.

The most troubling thing, however, was the fact Grace wanted to be involved. He didn't know if he'd be able to cope with that or not. Being around her stirred up too many painful memories. She'd broken his heart, and it had taken him years to get to the place where he was now. All he could do was protect himself so it didn't happen again. He didn't intend to ever let anyone hurt him again the way she had.

TWO

Even with the bright lights on the set, a chill rippled through Grace's body as she watched the footage from the bridge play on the monitor. She and Derek had reviewed the final cut several times, but her heart still hammered every time she watched her struggle to keep from going over the railing.

When the footage ended, the camera focused back on the WKIZ News anchor desk. Her coanchor Todd Livingston turned to her and flashed his trademark toothy smile. "Wow, Grace. You had quite a morning. Thank goodness that detective was there to keep you from being pulled over the railing."

Grace returned his smile. "Yes, Todd. It was touch-and-go there for a few minutes, but thanks to Detective Crowne, I wasn't hurt."

His gaze dropped to the elastic bandage around her wrist. "What did the doctor say about your arm?"

She held up her arm. "It's just a sprain. It should be okay in a few days. I really am lucky."

Todd looked into the camera and broadened his smile. "Knowing you, I doubt if you'll let a little thing like a sprained wrist slow you down."

She chuckled. "No, I won't. Before Mr. Mitchell plunged to his death, I promised him I would look into his son's death and see what I could find."

Todd turned back to her, his eyes wide. "But I thought you said his son committed suicide."

"The police suspect suicide, but they can't be sure. There was blood on the front seat. Mr. Mitchell believed his son was murdered and that the scene was staged to look like a suicide."

"So, what happens if you find something that suggests it might have been murder?"

"That's a matter for the police, of course. I've already talked with Detective Alex Crowne of the Cold Case Unit, and he's agreed to investigate the case with me." She looked into the camera. "If there's anyone who has information about Landon Mitchell's death or a high school secret society that he might have been a member of, you can contact me here at the station. Even if it's something that seems inconsequential, get in touch with me. You never can tell what detail might help to solve a crime."

Todd picked up the papers in front of him and shuffled them into a neat stack. "Well, that's all the time we have for today." He glanced at Grace and gave an exaggerated shiver. "Suicide on the Memphis-Arkansas Bridge? A secret society in one of our high schools? A twelve-year-old unsolved death? It sounds like my busy bee coanchor has enough to keep the newsroom buzzing for a while. Tune in tomorrow and see what she has for us next."

Grace plastered a smile on her face and held it until the camera shut down. Then she turned to Todd. "Were you trying to embarrass me on air?"

His eyes grew wide. "Why should I do that? You do it quite well without any help from me."

Her skin warmed, and she scooped up the papers on the desk in front of her. "What is that supposed to mean?"

Todd pushed to his feet. "Nothing. I just can't imagine a story about a secret society of high school kids in the most prestigious school in the city going on a killing spree. I have better stories to focus on than something like that."

Grace rose and faced him. She tilted her head to one side and smiled. "You know, Todd, I figured out a long time ago what the difference was between the two of us. We both love to report the news. But all I want is to keep the public informed about what's going on in the world. You, on the other hand, only care how you can use your reports to propel you to a network job."

Anger flashed across his face, but it disappeared when he noticed the cameramen were listening to their conversation. He took a deep breath and flashed his smile again. "And maybe it will, Grace. You might have blown your chance with the networks, but I haven't yet."

Grace watched Todd walk away before she turned to leave the set. Derek shook his head and pointed to Todd's retreating figure. "Don't let that guy get under your skin, Grace. He's jealous that you get more fan mail than he does. Everybody here at the station knows the reason you left your job in New York, and they admire you for coming back to help take care of your father after he was wounded in that drive-by shooting. We really respect you for that, Grace."

Her heart thudded as it did every time she thought of her active father confined to a wheelchair for the rest of his life. "Thanks, Derek. My family means a lot to me."

"I know that, but you need to watch your back. Todd made life miserable for his last coanchor before you came. He wants to anchor alone, and he wants to be in a bigger market." He stuck his hands in his pockets, observed Todd as he walked away and chuckled. "I sure do wish he would get a job at another station. Everybody here would be a lot happier."

Grace laughed. "Me, too, but I don't have time to worry about Todd today. We have an interview with the mayor this afternoon. Are you ready to go?"

"Yeah, do you want to grab a bite of lunch and head on downtown to his office?"

"I'm going to get my hair cut on my lunch hour today. I'll meet you there at two. Okay?"

"Sounds good to me. I'll see you then."

Grace hurried back to her office and had just grabbed her purse when her cell phone rang. Caller ID identified it as a private number, and she frowned. She sat down behind her desk and pulled the phone to her ear. "Hello."

"Grace, I saw your broadcast on the noon news. I thought we needed to talk."

Although the voice sounded familiar, she couldn't identify it. The thought crossed her mind that the caller was using some sort of voice distortion. "Who is this?"

"For personal reasons I'd like my identity to remain a secret. I'm sure you have anonymous callers a lot in your work. Just think of me that way—a nameless caller who wants to help you."

Grace took a deep breath. "Okay, but how did you get my private cell phone number?"

"It really doesn't matter. I called because I think you need to be careful."

Grace's hand tightened on the phone. "What's that supposed to mean?"

"It means that there are people who don't want you to get too close to the truth. Leave the past alone. You'll only end up getting hurt if you dig into Landon's death."

Grace gasped. "That sounds like a threat. Are you trying to scare me?"

"No, I'm warning you."

"Do you have some information about Landon's death?"

"Yes."

Grace sat up straighter in her chair and pressed her cell phone harder against her ear. "Was he murdered?"

"Please, Grace, for your own good, let it go."

"I can't let it go. Landon was my friend, and from the way you're talking, he was your friend, too. Don't you want people to know the truth?" He didn't answer for a moment, and she feared he'd disconnected the call. "Are you still there?"

She heard a heavy sigh. "All right. I tried to persuade you, but you haven't listened. If you're determined to continue, I see there's nothing I can do to discourage you. I have something I want to give you."

Grace's eyes grew wide. "I'll meet with you. Just tell me where and when."

"No, I don't want to do that."

"Then mail it to me."

"I suppose I could...." His voice trailed off. Then he inhaled. "No, I'll leave it for you somewhere."

She frowned. "Where?"

"I—I don't know. Somewhere that no one else would find it unless they were specifically looking for it. I'll think about it and let you know where to look. I'll call you again."

Grace's heart beat faster. She couldn't let him hang up before he'd agreed to give her his information. "Wait, don't go yet. Tell me where to look, and I'll do it."

He was quiet for a moment. "I remember hearing you say once that you are a geocacher."

"Yes, I am."

"And you said you like puzzle clues that lead to the hidden cache."

Grace frowned. "Yes, but I don't understand what that—"

"Has to do with finding Landon's killer?" Grace's skin prickled at the sudden change in the caller's voice. Moments ago it had been soft and reassuring. Suddenly it had become harsh and demanding. "You don't understand a lot of things, Miss Kincaid. If you want to find Landon's killer, you're going to have to solve much more than a geocache puzzle. I'm looking forward to seeing how smart you really are."

Grace stood up and gripped the phone tighter. "Don't threaten me, Mr. Anonymous. You may find out I'm a lot smarter than you thought."

"I doubt it."

Grace chuckled. "I get it now. You didn't call to warn me off. You wanted me more intrigued with this investigation than ever. If that was your plan, it seems to have worked. No way am I going to give up until I find out the truth."

He laughed, and the piercing tone chilled her. "Aren't you a little afraid of me?"

Her breath hitched in her throat, and her hand holding the phone shook. "N-no."

A laugh echoed in her ear. "Yes, you are. I can hear it in your voice. You'd be wise to be very afraid of me. You have no idea what's about to come down on you. Look for my instructions. Game on, Miss Kincaid."

Before she could ask another question, the call disconnected. She stared at her phone for a moment and debated whether or not she should call Alex. He'd asked her to let him know if she found out anything. So far the only thing she knew was that someone wanted to play some kind of game with evidence he claimed to have about Landon's death and he wanted her scared of him.

If her shaking legs were any indication, being afraid of him wasn't going to be a problem, but she couldn't give up now. She might have just talked to Landon's killer. Alex probably wouldn't agree, though. He would more likely think she'd received a call from some prankster who pretended to have information, but she wasn't so sure.

A cold chill ran up her arm at the memory of the voice on the phone. He said he heard her on the broadcast. Maybe she shouldn't talk about the investigation on the air. From now on, she'd be careful what she said. There were a lot of crazy people in the world, and the last thing she needed was to become the target of one.

Alex tossed the file he'd been studying down in front of him, propped his arms on his desk and buried his face in his hands. What was the matter with him? He'd been tense ever since he came into the office. Maybe he hadn't gotten over watching a man jump to his death, but in his heart he knew that wasn't true.

The main reason he'd been distracted all morning was because he couldn't quit thinking about Grace. He'd put their past behind him years ago, and now she wanted them to work together to investigate Landon Mitchell's death. Even though he'd agreed, he wasn't sure he was ready to do that. They would have to see each other from time to time, and that could stir up a lot of old memories that needed to be forgotten.

He pushed to his feet, let out a ragged breath and ran his hand through his hair. Maybe some lunch would make him feel better. Before he could turn and leave the office, the door opened, and his partners, Brad Austin and Seth Dawtry, walked into the room. Brad held a sack with the name of Alex's favorite fast food place printed on the side.

"Seth and I were downtown and had lunch. We stopped and picked something up for you since you were holding the office down."

Alex grinned, reached for the sack and sank back into his chair. "Thanks. I was about to go get something. Now I can eat at my desk."

Brad nodded. "We thought you might not be in the mood to go out. You've had a tough morning."

Alex sighed. "Yeah, it's never easy seeing someone commit suicide."

Brad and Seth exchanged glances. "Well, if you need to talk, buddy, we're here for you."

"Thanks, guys, I appreciate it, but I'm okay."

Brad opened his mouth to say something but shook his head, walked to his desk and dropped down in his chair. Seth considered Alex for a moment before he ambled over to his desk. When his partners appeared engrossed in what they were doing, Alex relaxed in his chair and pulled the burger and fries from the bag. He picked up a French fry, dredged it in catsup and shoved it in his mouth.

The thought of the look on Mr. Mitchell's face as he plummeted toward the river flashed in Alex's mind, and he frowned. He tried to chew the French fry he'd just put in his mouth, but he might as well have been eating sawdust for all the taste he got out of the piece of potato. He swallowed the fry, picked up the remainder of his lunch and put it back in the bag for later. There was no point in forcing himself to eat when his stomach churned. Maybe he needed to stop by the drugstore on his way home this afternoon and get something for a queasy stomach.

The problem was he'd had this feeling for years. It recurred every time he saw Grace, and he'd never found any medicine that could cure what ailed him. All he had to do was keep his distance from her, and after a few days he'd feel better.

After a few minutes he pushed to his feet. "I'm going to the break room for a cup of coffee. Anybody want anything?"

Brad and Seth shook their heads, and he strode from the room. He'd only taken a few steps down the hall when he heard music drifting from the break room. He stopped, glanced down at his watch and grimaced. Just his luck. It was time for the WKIZ noon news. He hesitated at the door, unsure if he should enter or turn and walk back to his office. He rubbed his hand over his eyes, took a deep breath and walked inside.

Several officers sat on the couch that faced the television, and their gazes were locked on the picture that filled the screen. Grace sat behind the anchor desk and in her usual professional manner related the events of the morning as she looked into the camera.

He couldn't move as she switched to the video the cameraman had filmed on the bridge. He shoved his hands into his pockets, leaned up against the door frame and watched in fascination as she reported the lead-in story for the newscast. His throat tightened, and his heart thudded as he relived each terrifying moment.

Perspiration dotted his forehead, and he reached up to wipe it away.

One of the officers glanced up and saw him standing in the doorway. "Hey, Crowne. That was some rescue you pulled off. I didn't know you could move that fast." The officers looked at each other and chuckled.

Alex pushed to his full height and managed a weak smile. "I just wish I could have saved Mitchell, but at least Grace Kincaid didn't go over the side, too."

He glanced back at the screen as the camera focused on Grace's face again. Behind her he could see red poinsettias arranged on shelves. As he studied her sitting among the holiday decorations on the set, he was reminded of Christmas their senior year in college. He couldn't wait for her to get back to Memphis from Philadelphia that year, but it hadn't turned out to be the happy time he'd anticipated. Instead, it had ended with his heart broken. Every Christmas since then had held little interest for him.

After a moment he stepped into the room and dropped down in a chair. He sat through the rest of Grace's newscast, but he didn't leave when the program was over and the other officers had returned to their desks.

Suddenly he felt tired. Maybe the morning's

events were just catching up with him. He leaned his head back, closed his eyes and drifted on the edge of sleep. The ringing of his phone jerked him awake, and he sat up straight. He had no idea how long he'd been in the break room.

He sat up and pulled his phone from his pocket. "Hello."

"Alex, this is Grace. Are you all right? You sound groggy."

He closed his eyes and rubbed his hand over them. "I'm alone in the break room, and I must have nodded off. The phone woke me. Why are you calling?"

She hesitated a moment. "I don't know if it means anything or not, but I just had a strange phone call."

He sat up straighter. "What do you mean?"

"Someone called and wouldn't tell me who it was. He said he has something he wants me to see."

"So you think he must have some information about Landon's death?"

"I do, but as the conversation progressed, he became sinister."

Alex rubbed the back of his neck. "Did he say he would call again?"

"No. He said he was going to hide whatever

it is he has and he'll send me a clue where it is. I thought you should know."

He nodded. "I'm glad you called. Did he say anything else?"

She hesitated a moment. "He said I should be afraid of him."

Alex exhaled and shook his head. "I don't like the sound of that. Be careful, Grace. Don't go to the parking lot alone when you leave work, and watch for anybody following you. Let me know if you hear from him again or if you receive anything from him."

"I will. I'll talk to you later."

He disconnected the call and sighed. This was what he'd been afraid would happen. The calls were already beginning to come. Whether or not this one was legitimate remained to be seen. But no matter, Grace's first thought had been to call him, and she'd probably do the same the next time something occurred that might affect the investigation.

The last thing he needed in his life was to spend time with Grace Kincaid, but it seemed that's where he'd been headed ever since Timothy Mitchell decided to jump off the bridge. All he could do now was guard against renewing any kind of friendship with Grace. He was determined that wasn't going to happen.

THREE

Grace pulled her car into her reserved parking spot at the television station and turned off the engine, but for some reason, she couldn't make herself get out. She didn't know if it was driving through the heavy morning traffic or her lack of sleep the night before that had left her feeling exhausted. She rubbed her hands over her eyes and tried to blot out the picture that had flashed in her mind during her sleepless night. Every time she'd closed her eyes, the scene on the bridge had popped into her mind. She saw herself grasping the bridge railing and staring down into Mr. Mitchell's wild eyes.

Her wrist throbbed, and she massaged it. A shiver went up her spine. No matter how hard she'd tried, she couldn't dispel the fear that flowed through her every time she thought of that moment.

She shook her head, took a deep breath and climbed out of the car. Thinking about what might have been was doing her no good. Today she would be thankful she was alive. She said a quick prayer of thanks as she headed into the building and down the hallway to her small office.

The minute she walked in the door she spotted the small box wrapped in brown paper on her desk. Her name and the address of the station were on the mailing label, but there were no stamps on the package. This had not come through the mail.

She was about to pick it up when a voice at the door startled her. "I see you found your delivery."

Grace whirled to see Julie Colter, a new employee, standing in the doorway. "Good morning, Julie. Did you see who delivered this?"

"Yes, it was a private messenger service. The guy asked if I would give it to you and I said I would."

Grace frowned. "Did you sign that you'd received the delivery?"

Julie shook her head. "No, he was gone before I had a chance to ask him."

Grace sighed. "Do you know the name of the messenger service?"

Julie thought for a moment before she shook her head again. "No, he just said it was a special delivery for you. I guess I assumed he was from a service." Julie's eyebrows rose, and her face turned red. "Did I do something wrong, Miss Kincaid?"

Grace hesitated before she answered. "Sometimes our newscasts can upset some people. We don't know who might send something harmful to us. We just need to be careful when accepting deliveries."

Tears welled in Julie's eyes, and she bit down on her lip. "Oh, Miss Kincaid, please don't tell the station manager I did anything wrong. I need this job. If he fired me, I don't know what I'd do."

Grace reached out and patted Julie's arm. "Now, now. Don't get upset. Nobody's going to get fired. You just need to be more careful in the future."

Julie nodded. "I will. I promise. Now, is there anything I can do for you?"

"No, thank you."

Julie eased toward the door. "Then I'll get back to work, and I promise I won't make that mistake again."

Grace nodded and didn't speak as the girl left the room. How many mistakes had Julie made since she was hired? It seemed the subject of Julie and her mishaps came up in the conversation no matter who you talked to at the station. She probably wouldn't make it much longer if her work didn't improve.

After a moment Grace turned her attention back to the package on her desk. Did it contain the clue her anonymous caller had told her about the day before? She leaned closer and studied the name and address on the mailing label. They had been typed, not handwritten, and there were no strings tied around the box, just tape to hold the paper.

Should she open it or not? Only a year ago a Memphis accountant had been injured when he opened an package that contained a bomb. Perhaps she should have Alex take a look at it or even dust it for fingerprints, but she would feel foolish if there was nothing threatening inside the envelope.

She pulled the tape loose and stepped back, then chuckled. If the box contained a bomb, a few steps away from the desk wouldn't be enough distance to offer any protection. She eased back to the desk and loosened the package's paper. It fell away to reveal a square box that looked to be about eight inches on each side.

Her heart pounded as she lifted the top of the box and peered inside. A folded piece of paper lay atop something wrapped in tissue paper. Frowning, she pulled the note out and unfolded it.

Dear Miss Kincaid,
I enjoyed our chat yesterday, and I have done as I promised. I have enclosed directions inside this box for the first stop on your journey. For a knowledgeable geo-cacher like you the puzzle should be no problem. Solve it, and you will find what I have left for you somewhere in the city. I will be watching to see if you are successful. I'm looking forward to our journey together as you find out the truth about Landon's death.
Your Anonymous Friend

The words made Grace's skin prickle, and she read the note several times before she reached in the box and pulled out the tissue-wrapped object. She tore the paper away and blinked her eyes in surprise at the six-sided puzzle cube she held. She slowly turned it and studied the twisty puzzle's mixture of white, red, blue, orange, green and yellow squares. Someone had turned the faces many times to make sure the colors were thoroughly mixed over every surface.

Something written on one of the white squares caught her eye, and she stared closer at it. Her breath hitched in her throat. A quick glance over the other surfaces told her that more white squares had markings. GPS coordinates! Her caller had just sent her a challenge. Solve the puzzle by arranging all the white cubes on one side and she would have a location where she would find a clue about Landon's killer.

She dropped down in her desk chair and began to twist the faces of the puzzle in an attempt to get all the white-colored surfaces on one side. After twenty minutes she was ready to throw the toy in the trash can. She'd played with these puzzles when she was growing up and never had mastered the art of getting all the sides back in order. She doubted if she could do it now.

"What are you doing?" Todd stood in the doorway to her office. A smirk pulled at his lips, and he let his gaze drift back and forth from her face to the puzzle in her hand. "Don't you have anything better to do than play with toys? We do have a noon newscast to do, you know."

Grace opened her desk drawer, shoved the puzzle inside and stood. "I like to keep my mind sharp, Todd. You might try doing that sometime yourself."

He glared at her and took a step forward. "Someday you're going to go too far with me, Grace."

She ignored the remark and crossed her arms. "Do you need something?"

Todd shook his head. "No, I just thought I'd check and see if you'd had any response to your plea on yesterday's newscast for information about Landon Mitchell's death."

"I haven't had anything concrete yet."

He cocked one eyebrow. "But you have had something?"

She shook her head. "Nothing I can talk about."

He pursed his lips and frowned. "Okay. Let me know if I can help you with anything."

"I will."

She waited until he'd left before she sank back in her chair. Nothing would please Todd better than to scoop her on the story of Landon's death. She would have to be more careful in the future.

Grace pulled the drawer open and looked down at the puzzle. She should call Alex. She'd promised to let him know if she heard anything from her mysterious caller. She jumped up, hurried to the door and closed it before she returned to her desk and dialed Alex's cell phone. He answered on the first ring.

"Hello, Grace."

The abrupt tone of his voice startled her, and she winced. "My, my. Don't you sound grouchy this morning?"

"I'm sorry. It's already been a busy morning." His voice softened. "How are you feeling?"

"Better today."

"Good."

"I don't know if it means anything or not…" Her office door rattled as if someone was about to open it. She paused in speaking. "Hold on a minute."

She rose, walked to the door and pulled it open, but there was no one there. She stepped into the hallway and caught a glimpse of Todd just as he disappeared around the corner at the end of the hall. Had he been listening outside her door?

Frowning, she stepped back into her office and closed the door. "I'm sorry. I thought someone was at the door, but I was wrong. But the reason I called was to let you know I received a message from my caller this morning."

"Really?"

He remained silent as she related the details of her delivery this morning and her inability to solve the puzzle. "He told me this wasn't going to be easy, and he was right. So, I'm at a standstill. I don't know where to go until I get the GPS coordinates arranged on one side of the puzzle."

"This sounds weird to me, Grace. But then I've never done any geocaching. I've heard about it, and I know it's like an internet scavenger hunt. But I really don't know how it works."

She chuckled. "It doesn't seem like something you'd be interested in, but I love it. Like you said, it's an international internet scavenger hunt that's run from a website. A cache is usually a small item that can be placed along with a log book in a box or some other container and hidden aboveground. Then the person who's hidden the cache logs the coordinates on a geocaching website, and hunters enter the coordinates in a GPS to search for them."

"So the searcher gets to keep the treasure when he finds it?"

"Not necessarily. The geocacher signs the log book that's been left at the cache site and may take the item inside or leave it. If they choose to take the item, they are required to leave something of equal value for the next hunter to find. When they return home, they log into the website and report the date they found the cache. It's not about what's found in the box. It's all about the hunt. I spend a lot of my weekends looking for caches. It tests your mind, and you get a lot of exercise, too."

Alex was silent for a moment. "So whoever sent you this puzzle is familiar with geocaching, and he knows you are, too. He's left you a clue to Landon's death, and the only way you can find it is to solve the puzzle and get the coordinates. Then you'll know where to look."

"That's right. I told you I would call if I found out anything, but I have no idea whether or not I'll ever be able to get the puzzle faces turned so that all the whites are on one side."

"I was never much good at working those things, either. If you solve it, give me a call, and I'll go with you to the location. I don't want you going by yourself."

Grace sighed. "Okay, I'll let you know, but don't hold your breath. This may be a hopeless task."

"Thanks for calling, Grace, and keep in touch."

"I will."

Grace opened her desk drawer, picked up the puzzle, and twisted the surfaces. The longer she worked the more hopeless the task appeared. After about twenty minutes, she tossed the cube on her desk and rose to her feet. She might as well give up.

She placed her hands on her hips and looked

down at the innocent-looking toy on her desk. Hidden on its surfaces were directions to a place that might reveal an answer to how Landon died. She had to get those coordinates lined up.

An idea hit her, and she smiled. There was more than one way to find what she needed to know. She sat down at her computer and pulled up the internet. Within minutes she had the information she needed.

She rushed to the hallway and hurried to the small closet near the staff restroom where the custodian kept his tools. She grabbed a screwdriver, took it to her office, and sat down at her desk. Smiling to herself, she picked up the cube and followed the instructions she'd found on the internet. First she rotated the top layer by 45 degrees, and pried one of its edge cubes away from the other two layers. The piece fell to her desk.

One by one she pulled the small cubes away from the center axis of the toy and watched them tumble to her desk in a pile of colors. When they were all stripped from the cube, she laid the white stickered sides out as if they were one surface on the cube and studied them. Frowning, she rearranged the pieces until she was satisfied she'd finally gotten the correct latitude and longitude. Then she leaned forward, folded her arms on top of her desk and smiled.

The coordinates stood out from the white surfaces. All she had to do now was enter them in her GPS and she would be on her way to finding out the truth about Landon Mitchell's death. Smiling, she picked up her cell phone and punched in Alex's number. He answered on the first ring.

"Hi, Grace."

"I've figured out the coordinates."

"Already?"

She laughed. "Well, to tell the truth I took a short cut. I tore the cube apart and laid the white sides out until I had the numbers in the right order."

"That was smart. When do you want to go take a look at the cache site?"

She glanced at her watch. "It's almost time for the noon news. What if I pick you up at the police station about one-thirty?"

"Sounds good. See you then."

Grace disconnected the call and sat there a few minutes. Ever since she'd been back in Memphis, she'd tried to avoid seeing or talking with Alex. Then yesterday they'd been reunited by a man who wanted them to bring out the truth about his son's death. Although she wanted to uncover the facts, she still wasn't sure working with Alex was a good idea. Once she'd trusted

Alex with all her heart, but when she'd needed him to have faith in her, he had failed her.

Her skin warmed at the thought of what Alex had said when he'd accused her the day before of wanting a story that would get her back to the networks. Although she'd denied it to Todd, in her heart she knew she hadn't really left that life behind.

Her primary reason for returning to Memphis had been to help her mother with her invalid father, but he was getting stronger every day. Maybe she could go back sometime in the future. That's why she couldn't let herself get sidetracked by old memories about Alex Crowne.

She glanced up at the clock on the wall and gasped. Thinking about what the future held for her would have to wait. Right now she had the noon broadcast to do. She picked up a pen and wrote the coordinates on a piece of paper, stuck it in an envelope and along with the puzzle pieces dropped it in her desk drawer.

Alex consulted the GPS unit Grace had handed to him when he got into her car and then looked at the traffic in the lane beside them as they drove along East Parkway. "You need to change lanes. We're going to turn left onto the road that leads down to the Overton Park Pavilion up ahead."

Grace nodded and glanced in her mirrors before she eased into the left lane and put on her turn signal. "Thanks."

She hadn't said much since she'd picked him up. He wondered if it was because she was intent on finding the clue her caller said he'd left or if it was because he was with her. He shook the thought from his head and sat silent as she turned onto the road leading into the park and drove toward the parking lot at the pavilion.

When she pulled to a stop in the deserted parking lot, she glanced around. "Not many people out today."

He let his gaze drift over the pavilion and nodded. "It's almost Christmas, Grace, and the temperature is in the thirties. Not a good day to be having a picnic in the park."

Her face flushed, and she smiled. "Yeah, I guess I'm so excited about finding the cache that I wasn't thinking." She took a deep breath and reached for the door handle. "I guess there's no use waiting. Let's go."

They climbed from the car, and Alex waited until she had joined him. He held the GPS unit so that she could see it and pointed toward the line of trees at the back of the pavilion. "It looks like we need to go there. I hope your caller thought it was too cold to get very far away from the pavilion."

She smiled and pulled her coat tighter. "You should have been born in the tropics. You never did like the Memphis winters."

The memory of the two of them building a snowman in the yard of her home when they were about ten years old crossed his mind, and he smiled. "That's not true. I like some things about winter. Low temperatures don't happen to be one of them."

"Then let's get this hike over with as quickly as we can."

Together they set off toward the trees in the distance. They didn't speak as they entered the Old Forest State Natural Area of the park and ducked under some low-hanging bare tree branches. Within minutes they'd walked so far they could no longer see the pavilion. Alex plodded along, his feet growing colder by the moment, and kept his eyes on their coordinates.

Finally, he held up his hand. "This is it."

Grace stopped, propped her hands on her hips and looked around. "It has to be around here somewhere. It could be at the base of one of the trees or partially hidden under a rock. It can't be underground but somewhere that can be easily found."

Alex pointed to the right of where they stood. "I'll take the area over here, and you take the opposite side."

She nodded and turned away from him. For the next few minutes they inched their way around the area as they inspected the trunks and bases of the trees. Alex turned rocks over and inspected each low-hanging branch to see if anything was perched there. He had just finished replacing a large rock he'd picked up when Grace called out. "I have something here."

He jumped to his feet and arrived at her side just as she pulled a small box out of a hole that had rotted away at the base of a tree trunk. She stood and held up the small container. "Here it is."

"It's not a very big box."

She shrugged. "It's not always about the size. It's about what's inside."

Grace loosened the string tied around the box, pulled the top off and found a small sealed envelope lying on top of a folded piece of paper. She slid her finger beneath the flap to unseal it and shook the contents into her hand. Her eyes grew wide, and she gasped at the sterling-silver ring that fell into her palm.

Alex leaned closer and frowned. "What is it?"

Grace swallowed and struggled to speak. She held it up for him to see. "It's a friendship ring."

"Does this have some special meaning for you?"

She nodded. "Yes, Landon gave it to me for my sixteenth birthday." She pointed to the top of the ring. "He picked it out because it was designed with the infinity symbol across the top with our two birthstones set in it. He said it would always make me think of him."

Alex looked at the ring again, then back to her. "Then what's it doing here?"

"I don't know. When Landon and I quit dating, I gave him the ring back. He had changed so much I didn't want anything to remind me of him. He told me someday I would want to come back to him, and until then he was going to wear the ring on his pinkie finger. Every time I saw him in the hall at school he would have it on and would hold up his hand for me to see."

Alex frowned. "Do you think he might have been wearing it when he died?"

"After his body washed ashore, I asked his father if he was wearing the ring. I wanted to keep it to remember him by, but his father said it wasn't on his body. Do you think the killer could have taken the ring off his finger and kept it all these years?"

Alex shrugged. "It's possible. Some killers like to keep some item from their victims. But why would he want you to know he had this ring?" He glanced at the box she still held. "What is that in the bottom of the box?"

She pulled the paper out and unfolded it. "It's a note."

Alex eased closer. "What does it say?"

"'Good afternoon, Miss Kincaid. Congratulations on solving the puzzle and finding the first clue in your quest to discover how Landon really died. I thought you might like to have the ring I've kept all these years. As you know, it meant a lot to Landon. Now you must decide if you want to find out how I got it. If you want to know, then you must solve the next clue in hopes it will bring you the answers you desire. Does your search end here, or are you tempted to continue? The next move is yours, but be prepared for whatever may come.'"

Alex pulled the note from her hand and scanned it before he looked at her. "Is there nothing else inside?"

She glanced back in the box and pulled out another folded sheet of paper. "Here's something."

She opened it and rolled her eyes in disgust. "It's a Sudoku puzzle."

"What? Let me see that." He glanced over the printed grid. "I see he's left the instructions for you at the bottom. Once you've solved the puzzle, you'll find the coordinates to the next clue in the sixth line across." He scanned the page for a moment before he looked back at Grace. "He's giving you clues instead of telling you what you want to know. I don't like this. He's taunting you, Grace. You need to stop this right now."

She shook her head. "But we have to keep looking into this, Alex. This guy knows something, or he wouldn't have this ring. He has to be the killer."

Alex shook his head. "Not we, Grace. This is getting out of hand. First he gives you an anonymous call, then he sends you a puzzle to find his hidden message, and when you do, there's another clue that threatens you. This guy is setting you up for something bad, and I don't like it. This is a matter for the police."

She glared at him. "No, I'm not giving up. I've been trained to follow a story wherever it goes. I'll keep working on this whether you help me or not."

"Grace, you're not listening to me. This is for your own good. I don't want to see you get hurt."

She snatched the note out of his hand and whirled. "I'm not going to get hurt. And I'm not giving up." She glanced over her shoulder as she stormed back through the forest.

He watched her go and shook his head in dismay. Yesterday Grace had accused him of being stubborn, but when she set her mind to something, she wouldn't give up. He kicked at a clump of dirt on the ground and took a deep breath.

She was determined to follow through on this, and he knew he'd do what he'd done ever since they were children. He'd be right there with her looking out for her. How could she still have a hold on him after all these years and after all they'd gone through? But she did, and he couldn't deny it. Maybe if he helped her with this case he could finally close the chapter on Grace Kincaid and put her out of his life permanently.

He jogged back through the forest to tell her he'd help her. When he emerged from the forest, he caught sight of her already in the parking lot. She stood next to her car, her cell phone to her ear. His skin prickled. Something wasn't right. As he got closer, he realized what it was. All four tires of her car had been slashed.

"Yes, the pavilion in Overton Park. I'm standing beside the car." She disconnected the call and turned as he came to a stop next to her. "I called the garage that I use. They'll take care of this and check to make sure no other damage was done before they deliver the car to my home later today."

"Good." He glanced around at the deserted parking lot. "I didn't see anybody when I came out of the forest. Did you?"

She nodded. "Just as I stepped out of the tree line, a car pulled out of the parking lot. At that distance I couldn't tell who was driving."

A gust of wind blew across the parking lot, and Alex shivered. "It's getting colder. I'll call Brad to come pick us up. Why don't we get in the car and wait for him there?"

She nodded. "That sounds good to me."

He walked over and opened the driver's door for her to step inside. Before she could move, the sharp crack of a gun split the quiet air, and a bullet slammed into the open car door. Alex lunged for Grace and knocked her to the ground as the second shot screamed over their heads.

"Get to the other side of the car," he yelled as he pulled his phone from the clip on his belt with one hand and his gun with the other. The shots appeared to have come from the forest. He fired in that direction, but he had no idea where the shooter was.

Grace scooted on her stomach to the far side of the car as shots continued to hit the side of her car. Alex crawled behind, his phone pressed to his ear as he fired off two more shots. "Officer under fire," he shouted into the phone. "Picnic pavilion at Overton Park. Need backup now!"

"Officers on their way." The 911 operator's voice crackled over the phone.

He grit his teeth and hoped they weren't too late as another bullet shattered the car's headlight. Fragments from the shattered headlight rained down on them as they scrambled to the far side of the car.

Alex sat up with his back pressed against the fender of the car and tried to peer around the front, but another bullet plowed into the front bumper. The gunfire seemed to be coming from a different direction. Maybe the shooter was working his way around so he had a clear shot at them now huddled beside the car.

Grace started to push up from the ground, but Alex shoved her back down and fell on top of her to shield her body as another bullet ripped past their heads. He was about to urge Grace to crawl to the back of the car when three police cruisers roared into the parking lot.

Before he could sit up, the officers, one of them holding a dog, jumped out of the cars, fanned out across the parking lot and headed toward the trees at the edge of the forest. Alex sat up and pulled Grace into a sitting position.

The lieutenant in charge of the officers squatted down beside them. "What happened here?"

Alex stood up and pulled Grace to her feet. "Thanks for getting here so quickly," he said as he began to relate the events in the park to the officer.

After about fifteen minutes one of the officers emerged from the forest and jogged to where they waited. "We searched the woods, sir. The dog hit on several places where the shooter had stood when he fired, but he was gone. He must have had his escape route planned well."

Alex nodded. "I could tell he was moving, trying to get a better shot."

"We're glad neither of you were hurt," the lieutenant said. His gaze traveled over the bullet-marked car and shook his head. "Too bad about the car. We're going to take another look in the woods before we go, but we'll be glad to give you a ride when we leave."

Alex shook his head. "No need for that. I'll call my partner." He pulled out his cell phone and punched in Brad's number.

Brad answered right away. "Hello."

"Brad, it's Alex. Grace and I are at the Overton Park Pavilion, and we need a ride. Can you come pick us up?"

"Sure, I'll be there right away."

"Thanks."

He disconnected the call and shoved the phone back in his pocket. "Brad should be here shortly. He can take you back to the television station. Would you like for me to give you a ride home this evening?"

"I'd appreciate it. I'll be ready as soon as the six o'clock news is over." A cold wind blew across the parking lot, and she drew her coat closer around her. She bit down on her lip and pointed to her car. "This doesn't change anything, Alex. I'm still going to pursue this story."

He gritted his teeth. "What's the matter with you? Are you crazy? Somebody just tried to kill us, and you want to keep going with this investigation? This is something for the police to address, not you."

"I don't understand why he waited until we got back to the car to shoot at us. He could have done that while we were in the forest."

Alex nodded. "I was wondering the same thing."

"What if he didn't intend to kill us? What

if he only wanted to scare us?" She pulled the note from her pocket. "I think he wants us to find the next clue."

"We could offer what-ifs all day long and not be any closer to the truth than we are now," Alex said. "The facts are that someone lured you to a deserted place then shot at you. Whether or not he meant to kill you doesn't matter. Any one of those bullets could have found their mark. This is where your involvement with this investigation has to end."

"No, it doesn't." Tears sparkled in her eyes, and she pulled Landon's friendship ring from her pocket and slipped it on her finger. "I'm convinced that whoever shot at us took this ring off Landon's finger after he killed him. I promised his father I would find out the truth, and I'm not giving up until I know what it is."

"Grace, please..."

"No! I won't give up even if I have to do this on my own."

He exhaled and shook his head. It would do no good to argue with her, and he'd come to the decision about what he should do while he was still in the forest. "I know I'm wasting my breath trying to get you to see reason, Grace. If you're determined, I'm not going to let you do this alone." He sighed and reached for the paper she still held. "I work these puzzles all the time. I'll get started on it tonight."

"Thank you, Alex." She hesitated a moment, and he knew she was about to ask him to do something else.

He groaned inwardly. "I know that look, Grace. What else do you want me to do?"

"When you take me home, I'd like for you to come inside and be with me when I tell my parents what happened today."

He shook his head. "I don't know, Grace. Your father never did like me. To him I'll always be the gardener's son. I doubt if my presence will make any difference."

"You're wrong. My father is very different from when you knew him, and I want you to see for yourself. Please do this."

He wanted to tell her no, but her eyes begged him to do this. After a moment, he nodded. "Okay, I'll come in for a few minutes."

She smiled. "Thank you, Alex."

She crossed her arms and leaned back against the car. Alex turned and stared into the woods where the officers continued to search. He glanced down at the broken headlights and the bullet holes in the car. They had barely missed being killed today.

Cold fear washed over him, and he rubbed the

hair on the back of his neck. Grace had opened a Pandora's box with her announcement on air that she was going to look into Landon Mitchell's death. There was nothing he could do to stop what might come, but one thing he could do was be there to make sure nothing happened to Grace.

FOUR

Grace gazed out the window of Alex's car as he drove toward her home on the outskirts of Memphis. Usually she enjoyed the ride home from work, but not today. She had tried all afternoon to push her brush with death from her mind, but she couldn't. She didn't know if she would ever forget how those bullets had sounded as they hit her car. Thankfully, neither she nor Alex had been hurt, but the experience wasn't one she would soon forget.

Now she had to get through another troubling time. She had to tell her parents. If she didn't, they might read about it in the paper or hear it on the news. With her father's condition, she didn't want him upset, but she didn't see any way around it.

She straightened in her seat as they approached the edge of her family's property. Alex pulled into the driveway of the house, stopped at the gate and swiveled in his seat to face her. "Is the security code the same or has it been changed?"

She smiled. "It's still the same."

Alex punched in the code and drove through the gates onto the grounds of the home where she and Alex had played as children while his father was working there. He drove forward and stopped in front of the sprawling house. "Here we are. Are you sure you want me to come in?"

"I am." She glanced down at her watch and opened the car door. "My parents may not be home yet. Dad had an appointment scheduled with a physical therapist for late this afternoon. I'm sure the cook has something for us to munch on while we're waiting for them. Come on inside."

Fifteen minutes later Grace and Alex sat on the sofa in the den and watched the blue gas flames flickering around the logs in the fireplace across the room. Grace set her coffee cup on the table at the end of the couch and turned to face Alex who sat at the other end. "I'm glad we have this time together before my parents get home. Everything has happened so fast for the past two days that we haven't had time to talk."

He set his cup down and exhaled. "Talk about what, Grace? I think we've probably said it all at one time or another."

"There are several things I'd like to say. First of all, I want to tell you about my father."

"What about him?"

She took a deep breath. "I want you to know what he's gone through in the past year. After the drive-by shooting he was in bed for a long time before he reached the point where he could be in a wheelchair. During that time the pastor of the church nearby visited him a lot and shared with him the things in life that are really important and how God can get you through the bad times. After a lot of Bible study and prayer, Dad turned his life over to God. Now he's trying to reach out to those he may have hurt in the past and apologize."

"B-but this is so unlike him. You're telling me that your father has become a believer?"

"I am. My mother and I are, too. My father's shooting has changed everyone in the Kincaid household. For the first time since I can remember, we're a real family. We also attend church every Sunday."

"Wow. I can't believe I'm hearing this."

She smiled. "It's true. Because I've put my trust in God, I've been able to get through a lot this past year, but there's one thing I know I have to do. I want to be friends with you again. I want you to forgive me for all the mistakes I made.

I'm praying you can do that, and I think this is the time to try. I don't want us to go on saying and doing things that hurt each other. I think it's time we called a truce, especially since you've saved my life twice since yesterday morning."

He shook his head. "I don't know if we can ever be friends again, Grace. I'm glad I was there to save your life, but I was only doing my job."

She blinked to keep the tears from filling her eyes. "I'd like to think it was a bit more personal than that. But even if it's not, we can't keep going through life pretending the other one doesn't exist."

He took a deep breath. "Now that you're back in Memphis, it's hard to pretend you don't exist. I see you on television nearly every day or I see your picture in the paper. I saw you on the society page not too long ago at a dinner at your country club, and also at a swanky party for the Cotton Carnival. You looked like you were surrounded by your friends."

She looked at him for a moment before she spoke. "I have lots of friends that I enjoy being with. I'd like for us to be friends again."

He pulled his gaze away from her and looked into the fireplace flames again. As she took in his profile, the muscle in his jaw twitched. "I don't think that's going to happen. There's too much history between us, Grace."

She swallowed the lump in her throat and leaned forward. "We can try." She closed her eyes for a moment and bit down on her lip. When she opened her eyes, he was staring at her again. "I don't expect us to ever go back to where we were that summer before our senior year in college. I want to go back to the children we were when I followed you everywhere."

He let his gaze drift around the room. His eyes locked on the Christmas tree with the presents piled underneath and shook his head. "I've never seen that many presents under one tree in my life. It's just one more reminder of the differences in our lives. We may have been childhood friends, but you were the daughter of the rich banker and I was the son of his gardener. It wasn't okay with your father for you to be my friend then, and it certainly wasn't when I got that scholarship to attend the same private school as you."

"You know I didn't care what my father thought. I was thrilled when you got that athletic scholarship and we got to see each other at school."

A snort of disgust rumbled in Alex's throat. "Yeah, we went to the same school, but I was never one of the guys." He grimaced. "Landon Mitchell and his friends never let me forget it."

Grace sank back against her chair. "I tried to tell you none of that mattered. Not to me, at least."

He shrugged. "Well, being accepted by the group matters to a high school kid, and it did to me. When I look back on it now, I see it from an adult's perspective, but it hurt back then."

"Did I ever make you feel like you weren't accepted?"

"No, but everything changed when you left for University of Pennsylvania and I stayed here at the University of Memphis. It was like I was free of all those childhood feelings and I was moving on with my life."

Grace sighed. "And then we ran into each other on Beale Street the summer before our senior years in college."

His eyebrows drew together, and he scowled. "There's no need for us to rehash all our history, Grace. To you it was a summer romance. To me it was more."

She clenched her fists in her lap and shook her head. "It was more to me, too. I really missed you that fall when I went back to school."

He rolled his eyes and glanced back at the blinking lights of the decorated tree. "Yeah, I sure had a merry Christmas that year when I found out you'd been making plans for us. You had the rest of our lives all planned out."

Her anger flared, but she tried to extinguish it. She would never be able to make Alex see the truth if she argued with him. "I didn't. I only wanted to take the chance to turn my internship at the Philadelphia television station into my first real job. They had offered me a good opportunity, one a new college graduate couldn't get anywhere else. You could be a cop anywhere."

His lips thinned, and he gritted his teeth. "I didn't want to be a cop anywhere. I wanted to be one right here in Memphis. I thought if you really loved me, you'd want me to work where I'd be the happiest."

"Ever since we were children, you'd done everything you could to make me happy. I thought if you could see what a great opportunity it was for me, you would give in and come to Philadelphia to work."

He shook his head. "You never understood how I love Memphis. It's where I was born and where I want to spend my life. In my job I've come to know the streets, the back alleys and the people who inhabit those places. I feel the music of Beale Street in my soul, and I love to watch the Mississippi River roll by. I could never feel that way about another place. I didn't want Philadelphia."

"So you made me choose."

He rubbed the back of his neck and sneered. "Yeah, and we both know which you chose—Philadelphia and all it offered for you. The boy who had loved you since he was ten years old was left behind without a second thought."

She shook her head. "No, you're wrong about that. I thought you'd change your mind after a while and come join me."

"And I thought you'd come back home. I waited a year for you, but you stayed in Philadelphia. Of course I found out it wasn't just the job. It was Richard Champion the news anchor that was so appealing to you."

Grace almost flinched from the anger in Alex's eyes. Could she ever make him understand what it had been like for her alone in Philadelphia? "All right. Let's talk about Richard. He was my mentor at the TV station when I was doing my internship, nothing more. When I started my job there after graduation, he was kind to me. He knew we had broken up, and he offered me a shoulder to cry on. Before I knew it, we were going out to dinner, taking in movies or just hanging out and talking. He was my friend."

Alex's eyebrows arched. "How long did the *friendship* last?"

"I waited a year for you, Alex, but you didn't come. By that time I had a job, and I liked it. When Richard asked me to marry him, I couldn't think of a reason to say no. We got along well, and we understood what the other one went through in our jobs. There was just one thing lacking, although I didn't realize it at the time."

"What was that?"

"I didn't love him."

He leaned forward and gazed at her. "You can't imagine what I went through thinking about you married to that guy. But what happened? That's part of the story I've always wanted to know. Why didn't you marry him?"

Grace swallowed hard and met his gaze. "Because two weeks before the wedding I caught him with the weather girl at the station. As it turns out, she was only one of the women he was having an affair with."

A look of surprise flashed on Alex's face, and he slumped back in his seat. "So that's why you went to New York to work instead of staying in Philadelphia."

"Yes."

"And now? Why did you really come home, Grace?"

"I'll be honest with you, Alex. I didn't want to quit my job in New York, but I did because I love my family. My father may be rich, but his money didn't help him any when he was shot. He's lucky to be alive even if he is confined to wheelchair for the rest of his life."

His features softened, and he nodded. "I was sorry to hear about that. I looked into the case after I joined the Cold Case Unit, but there weren't any leads. I wish I could have solved the case for you."

"I wish you could have, too." She took a deep breath. "When I first came back, Laura and I shared a house. After she and Brad married, my mother was having a difficult time, and I decided to move home. It was the best for all of us. I like my job at the station, and I come home to my family every night. It's not a very exciting life, but it's the one I have."

He didn't say anything for a moment, then he smiled. "Well, after what's happened the past two days, I'd say your life has just gotten a lot more exciting."

She laughed. "You can say that again." Her smile faded. "Do you think we can ever be friends again?"

He exhaled a long breath. "I don't know, Grace. I've spent the past five years angry at you for dismissing my feelings so easily. When I told you I loved you, I thought I could trust you with my heart. But you broke it, and I don't know if I can ever get the trust back I felt for you."

She nodded. "I understand. Now I know I was selfish and self-centered. I only thought of what I wanted. I never tried to come up with a compromise that could make us both happy. But then, neither did you."

"I guess we both failed. I guess we should chalk our romance up to one of those things that was never meant to be and go from there."

It surprised her to think that he might be right. She didn't know if her life would have been different if she'd never fallen in love with Alex, but at least she wouldn't have spent years getting over him. "I think it's time we put the past behind us and concentrate on what we're doing now. Maybe in discovering the truth about Landon's death, we can find our way back to being the friends we were when we were children."

He shook his head. "I don't know, Grace. Going back may be too difficult. But maybe we can at least be cordial to each other while we're working together."

She smiled. "Maybe so."

"Excuse me, Miss Kincaid."

Grace looked over her shoulder to see the maid standing in the doorway. "What is it, Nancy?"

"Your mother's car just drove into the garage.

You said you wanted to know when she arrived so you could help her get your father inside."

Grace jumped to her feet. "Thank you, Nancy. Tell her I'll be right there."

She turned back to Alex. "I'm glad we had this talk today." She glanced at her watch and frowned. "They're later than usual. I'm sure my father will be hungry and will want to eat right away. Why don't you stay for dinner?"

Alex rose from the sofa and shook his head. "No, I really should go."

Grace waved her hand in dismissal. "Don't be silly. My parents will be glad to see you. Besides, I really do need you with me when I tell them about today."

She held her breath as he appeared to debate whether or not to stay. After a moment, he nodded. "Okay, if you're sure it will be all right."

"Of course it is. Now sit back down and wait until I help get my father in the house. I'll be back in a few minutes."

Grace hurried from the room before Alex had time to think up another reason to leave. She dreaded telling her parents about the incident in the park, but it had to be done. Her father didn't need something else to worry about right now. He needed to concentrate on the therapy that was restoring some movement to his legs.

Her prayer every night was that someday her father would be able to stand again. She hadn't dared pray yet that he could walk, just stand. If he could do that, it would make walking possible.

She glanced down at the friendship ring on her finger and said a quick prayer that God would lead her to the person who had kept Landon's ring for the past twelve years. If she and Alex could find him, they might find that he and Landon's killer were one and the same.

Dinner was drawing to a close, and Alex hoped he could soon make his exit. All during the meal Grace had tried to downplay the events of the past two days as best she could. He couldn't believe how her account of their experience in the park had lacked certain details. To hear her tell it, someone had slashed her tires and shot up her car. She'd left out the part where she and Alex had been present and cowering beside the car as bullets whizzed past them. He had arched his eyebrows as she related her version of the story, and she had frowned and given a slight shake of her head.

Her father's piercing blue eyes bored into him. "Thank you, Alex, for what you did yesterday at the bridge and taking care of her car in the park. Our family is indebted to you."

A frown pulled at Alex's forehead, and he rubbed his hand across his face. He could hardly believe Grace's father was speaking to him like this. In the past he'd always treated Alex like someone beneath the social level of his family and had ignored him when they met. Now there was a warm tone to his words, and Alex found it difficult to associate it with the man he had once known.

"There's no need to thank me, sir. I was just doing my job. Of course, since it was Grace, I was especially thankful I was successful."

"And so are her mother and I." He hesitated a moment. "I know your father must be very proud of your rise through the ranks in the police department."

"He is, sir."

"Well, I'm happy for you, too, but I do miss your father since he retired to Florida. When you speak to him, tell him hello for me."

"I'll do that. He'll be glad to know you miss him."

As the maid removed the dessert plates, Mr. Kincaid pushed the controls on his wheelchair and backed away from the table. "Let's have coffee in the den."

Alex moved to the back of Mrs. Kincaid's chair, assisted her as she rose to her feet and smiled. "Thank you for a wonderful dinner, Mrs. Kincaid."

She patted his arm and looked up into his eyes. "It was a pleasure having you, Alex, and please call us Martha and Harrison."

He darted a quick glance in Grace's direction before he swallowed and nodded. "Thank you. I'd like that."

Harrison led the way as they left the dining room and headed toward the den. When they entered the den, the coffee service sat on the table in front of the sofa. Martha pointed to it as she sank into a chair next to her husband's wheelchair. "Grace, would you serve the coffee?"

Grace nodded, sat down on the sofa and picked up the silver coffeepot. Her hand trembled a bit when Alex settled next to her. She smiled and handed him the first cup. "Black, just the way you like it."

A small smile pulled at his lips as he took the cup. "I see you can remember some things better than others."

Grace ducked her head and nodded before she poured two cups for her parents. When they were finally served, Alex glanced at Grace's father. "You seem to be doing well handling your wheelchair, Mr. Kin— I mean Harrison."

He nodded and set his cup on the tray of the wheelchair. "Yes. It took a while to get used to the controls of this motorized contraption, but I think I have it mastered now. It's not like walking, but it gets me around."

"I'm glad to see you're doing so well."

Harrison pursed his lips before he spoke. "I don't think I'd be doing so well today if you hadn't been there to help Grace yesterday and today. I want you to know how grateful we are to you."

Alex set his cup down and shook his head. "You've already thanked me for what I did, but I'm glad I was there, too. I'm sure any other policeman would have done the same."

"They might have done the same, but it wouldn't have meant as much to me. Especially with our history."

Alex shook his head. "Please, there's no need…"

He held up and hand and interrupted him. "Oh, but there is. I've had a lot of time to think this past year, and some of the things I've remembered have troubled me a great deal. One of those things is how I acted toward you in the past. I never liked your coming here with your father, but I tolerated it because he was the best gardener I'd ever had and because I knew he didn't want to leave you home alone after your mother passed away. I'm afraid I wasn't very gracious to you, and I said things that must have cut deeply into a child's heart."

Grace stilled and glanced at Alex. A slight flush covered her cheeks. He took a deep breath. "You're right about that, but it's in the past."

"Then when Grace told me the two of you were in love," her father continued, "I behaved even worse. I'm saying all this tonight, Alex, because I now realize how wrong I was to judge you because of my misguided ideas about social position. I've wanted to tell you this for some time, and I'm glad you're here tonight so I can. I want to ask you to forgive me for how I've treated you in the past. I hope you can find it in your heart to do so."

After a moment, Alex swallowed. "I forgive you, Mr. Kincaid, and I thank you for telling me this. It means a lot to me."

Her father smiled. "Harrison, Alex. No more Mr. Kincaid."

A slow grin pulled at Alex's lips. "That may take some time, but I'll try."

Harrison let out a big breath. "Good. Now that's all taken care of, we can finish our coffee."

A rustling sound at the door alerted them that someone had entered, and Alex glanced over his shoulder at Nancy, the maid, who stood just inside the room. She looked at Grace. "Excuse me, Miss Grace, a man from Hammonds Garage is on the phone. He says he needs to talk to you about all the damage to your car."

Grace set her cup on the coffee table and jumped to her feet. "Thanks, Nancy."

Her father glanced at Grace. "All the damage? I thought you said it was just a few bullet holes."

She cast a frantic look at Alex who had also risen before she responded. "I'll, uh, go see what he has to say."

Her father shook his head. "No. I can tell you're hiding something from me. What's going on?" He moved his chair closer and glared at her. "I may be in a wheelchair, but I still have my mental faculties. Are you not telling me something?"

Grace glanced over at the maid. "Nancy, please tell Mr. Hammonds I'll call him later." She turned back to her father. "Please, Dad, the doctor has told us it's not good for you to get upset. I was only trying to spare you the details."

Her father grasped the arms of his wheelchair and gritted his teeth. "Grace, tell me what's going on."

Even in his present condition, Grace's father could still create a commanding presence. Alex had seen it many times, and tonight was no exception. Grace turned to him, a pleading look on her face. "Alex, help me out here...."

Alex took a deep breath. "I'm sure Grace didn't want to worry you by not telling you everything that happened in the park today. The truth is her car was bombarded with gunfire today while we were huddled behind it." His voice seemed to echo in the now-quiet room.

Her father's face paled, and his mouth hung open. Her mother bolted out of her chair. "What did you say?"

Alex glanced at Grace and sighed. "I'm sorry, Grace, but they deserve to know what happened."

"What are you talking about?" Mr. Kincaid's voice thundered across the room.

Grace started to protest, but Alex held up his hand. "No, Grace. They need to know the truth." Before she could protest again, he began to speak and didn't quit until he had told them everything that had happened since the incident on the bridge. "So," he concluded, "I think Grace needs to back away from this story and let the police handle it."

"And I think you're right," her father said.

"So do I," her mother added.

Grace clasped her hands in her lap and stared down at them for a few moments before she took a deep breath, rose slowly to her feet and looked at her parents. "I understand your concern, but I can't back down from this. You knew when I entered this type of work that I might be called on to report stories that would put me in danger, but that's one of the things that drew me to journalism. I love the excitement of following a story, and I want to find out what happened to Landon. He was my friend, and I think I owe it to him to find out the truth about his death."

Her mother's eyes filled with tears. "Even at the expense of worrying your parents?"

Grace hurried to her mother's side and grasped her hands. "I don't want to worry you and Dad, but this is something I have to do." She glanced back at Alex. "Besides, I'll be safe. Alex has agreed to help me."

Her father studied them for a moment before he shook his head. "Don't you understand? Sometimes we have no control over what happens to us. Look at me. I'm a prime example of that. I never thought I'd end up in a wheelchair, but here I am."

Grace stared down at her clutched hands in her lap. "Dad, please, don't get upset."

"No," he said. "You have to understand how quickly something can happen that will change your life forever. Nothing seemed out of the ordinary when I left my office the day I was shot. People were leaving their workplaces, and the street was filled with traffic. All of a sudden I heard the roar of a car and gunshots. It took a few seconds for me to realize I was on the ground and bleeding. Even with so many potential witnesses around, nobody could describe the car or the shooter. The police thought someone shot into the crowd, and I was the unlucky one hit. I don't want this or even something worse for you."

"Please, Dad, try to understand. This means a lot to me."

"Grace, your mother and I think—"

Alex stepped forward and interrupted. "I think you're wasting your breath. I've already tried to talk Grace out of this. But I promise you, I'll stick close to her and make sure nothing happens to her."

Grace mouthed the words *thank you* before she turned to her father. "See, Dad? Alex will be with me."

Her father exhaled a deep breath and nodded. "Very well then. I don't like it, but I'll feel better if Alex is with you. Please be careful. I don't think your mother and I could stand it if anything happened to you."

Grace bent over her father and kissed his cheek, then stepped beside her mother and did the same thing. "Thank you. I love you both so much. I promise I'll be careful."

Tears flooded her father's eyes, and he glanced at Alex. "Promise me you'll take care of my daughter, Alex."

Alex nodded. "I'll do everything in my power to keep her safe, sir."

"Good." He cleared his throat and glanced at her mother. "Now why don't you help me to my room, and we can leave these two young people alone?"

"You don't have to do that," Alex protested.

Her father shook his head. "No, I'm tired. I had a rough day with my therapist. I'm ready to go to bed." He smiled at them. "Good night, Alex. It was good to have you in our home, and, Grace, I'll see you in the morning."

Alex stood next to Grace as her mother followed the slowly moving wheelchair from the room. When the door closed, she turned back to Alex. "Thank you for supporting me."

He rubbed the back of his neck and shook his head. "I don't think I did you any favors. I'd feel better if you'd do what your father wanted and forget all about Landon Mitchell's death."

"I can't do that."

He studied her for a moment. "No, I guess you can't. You always went after what you wanted, and it didn't matter what anybody else said or if they got hurt as long as you got your way. You'd think after all these years I would have learned my lesson, but I guess I haven't." He exhaled and pulled the Sudoku puzzle from his pocket. "Why don't we work on this now?"

Before she could answer, he strode across the room, grabbed a chair and carried it to the desk by the window. After a moment she followed, and they sank down in the two chairs now at the desk.

Neither of them spoke. Then Alex laid the paper he held on the desk, pulled a pencil from a cup that held a variety of writing instruments and began to study the puzzle. Beside him Grace crossed her arms and fidgeted as the minutes went by, but she didn't say anything.

Grace's anger radiated out of her body like a blazing fire consuming everything in its path. Alex heard the intake of her breath and knew what that meant. He'd experienced enough of her lectures in the past to know. He dropped the pencil onto the desk and leaned back in the chair.

"Okay, let's have it."

She hesitated. "Have what?"

"The lecture you're about to deliver. What is it this time? I'm insensitive to your feelings, or I don't understand you or your opinion is never important to me? Which one is it? I've heard them all."

He turned to her, and his heart pricked at the tears she tried unsuccessfully to blink from her eyes. Her mouth opened as if she meant to speak, but she said nothing. Her shoulders drooped, and her body appeared to deflate. She didn't move but held her gaze steady on him. Finally, she frowned and slowly reached across until her hand rested on his arm.

"Was I really that awful, Alex? Did I make you feel like I thought I was superior?"

The sudden shift in her mood startled him, and he regretted the harsh tone he'd used with her. His skin grew warm where she touched him, and he had to force himself not to cover her hand with his. He swallowed as he stared at her. "Sometimes."

A tear escaped the corner of her eye and trickled down her cheek. "I'm so sorry. I didn't realize." She closed her eyes and shook her head. Then she reopened her eyes and looked at him with a sad expression that stabbed at his heart.

"I guess old habits are hard to break. I admit when I turned toward you a few minutes ago I was going to let you know that I wasn't the only one at fault when we broke up. We were young, and we wanted different things. We gave up too easily."

Alex pulled his arm toward him, and her hand released him. He rubbed his eyes and shook his head. "Yeah, but we had a lot going against us, Grace. You wanted a life away from Memphis and I didn't. Besides that, your family didn't like me." He sighed. "I guess it turned out all right in the end."

"It will turn out all right only if we can forgive each other and try to be friends again. Don't you want us to be able to be together without reliving all the hurts of the past?"

He didn't know how to answer her. He wished they could go back and capture the childhood friendship they'd had, but he didn't know if he could do that or not. However he felt, though, he had promised her father he would make sure nothing happened to her on her mission to find out the truth about Landon's death. But could his battered heart survive letting Grace back into his life? Alex and Grace together again. This time as friends. Nothing more.

Finally, he nodded. "I want to see if we can.

I promise I'll do my part, and I won't bring up the past again."

She smiled, and the light from the room's crystal chandelier reflected in the tears standing in her eyes. "I won't, either. We'll start anew tomorrow, and we'll concentrate on finding the answer to Landon's death. Maybe by working together we can achieve some kind of truce between the two of us."

He squeezed her hand and smiled. "Maybe so." He picked up the puzzle from the desk and pushed to his feet. "I think I'd better go now. We both have a lot to think about. I'll finish the puzzle and come by the TV station tomorrow."

She smiled and stood beside him. "That sounds good. Make it after lunch if possible. The mornings are hectic."

"I have no idea how long this will take me, but I won't come in the morning."

"I'll see you to the door."

They walked from the room with Alex right behind her. When Grace opened the front door, she smiled at him again. "Thank you for coming, Alex. You have eased my father's mind a lot. He's been so concerned that you wouldn't forgive him."

"I'm glad I came, too. I'd like to come see your father again sometime if he'd like."

"He would be thrilled. He gets very lonely."

Alex stepped outside and turned back to face Grace. "Then tell him I'll drop by from time to time to see how he's doing. Tell your mother thank you for the wonderful meal, and I'll see you tomorrow. Good night."

"Good night, Alex."

He walked to his car, which he'd parked in the circle driveway in front of the house, and got in. Grace stood in the doorway as he headed back to the main gate. Just before he got there, it opened, and he drove out onto the road. She must have opened it for him.

Alex settled back in his seat and glanced up at the bright Memphis skyline in the distance. He turned the car toward the city and smiled. All in all the evening had been a success, and he felt better than he had in a long time.

He patted the right side of his chest, and the puzzle paper inside his pocket rustled. Maybe this clue would give them some answers to Landon Mitchell's death. By tomorrow this time, he might be able to close a case that had been cold for twelve years. If they did solve the case, Alex had one regret—Landon's father wouldn't be there to know.

FIVE

With the noon newscast completed, Grace hurried off the set toward her office. She had almost reached her destination when she realized she wasn't alone. She stopped and turned to face Todd, who had followed her.

She crossed her arms and arched an eyebrow. "Is there something I can do for you, Todd?"

"I've been concerned about your injury and wanted to ask how you're feeling." He smiled, and she wondered why his trademark grin never quite reached his eyes. Perhaps it was because she'd seen him practicing the expression in front of a mirror from time to time. She wasn't about to be fooled by his insincere interest in her well-being.

Grace pasted a smile on her face. "I'm almost as good as new, but thanks for asking."

She turned to leave, but he took a step closer. "Any leads in the investigation of your friend's death?"

She shook her head. "Nothing yet, but don't

worry. If I learn anything, you'll be the *last* person I tell."

His smile disappeared, and anger flashed in his eyes. "Don't get smart with me. I simply asked you a question."

"A question?" She frowned at him and took his measure. "I thought you might know the answer already. I have a feeling you're keeping a close watch on me."

His face turned red, and his eyes grew wide. "I—I don't know what you're talking about."

"Oh, come on, Todd. I know you'd like to get out of Memphis, and you'd do anything to make it happen, even snatch a story right out from under one of your colleagues. I've heard the stories about what you did to your last coanchor, and I don't intend to let you do that to me."

He shook his head. "I could care less about your story. I can find my own without any help from you." His angry voice echoed down the hall, and several cameramen who were standing at the other end turned and stared at them. He stepped closer and lowered his voice. "You're making a big mistake if you think you scare me. I intend to go somewhere else, and I won't allow you or anybody else to stop me."

She studied him for a moment before she spoke. "I assure you I won't stop you from going, but let this be a warning to you, Todd. You stay away from me and from my story. I'm going to be watching to make sure you do. If you want to get to the networks so badly, do it on your own. Don't use my work as your stepping stone."

Before he could reply, she whirled and stormed down the hallway. When she rounded the corner leading toward her office, she came to an abrupt halt. Alex, his back to her and with his cell phone to his ear, leaned against the wall across from her office door. She drank in the familiar sight. A smile tugged at her lips when she noticed his hair touching his collar in the back. How many times in the past had she reminded him it was time to get a haircut?

"I'll check in with you later, Brad," she heard him say, and she shook her head to rid it of those troubling thoughts from the past.

Grace took a deep breath and stepped closer. "Hello, Alex. I wondered when you would come by."

He straightened to his full height and turned to face her. He smiled as he slipped his phone in his pocket. "Hi, Grace," he said. "I arrived while you were doing the newscast. Some girl named Julie offered to let me sit in your office, but I told her I'd wait in the hall."

Grace rolled her eyes as she pushed the door open. "Julie is new here. We're having a time training her in proper office procedures. She's very naive." She grinned at him and waved him to a chair as she sat down in her desk chair. "Of course I wouldn't have minded you waiting in here."

"No problem." He pulled the puzzle out of his pocket. "I finished this while I was having my coffee this morning. I have the coordinates."

She reached across the desk. "May I see it?"

He hesitated a moment. "I suppose I'm hoping you'll give up this search." When she didn't respond, he sighed and handed her the puzzle. "I've written the coordinates at the bottom of the page."

She nodded and studied the completed puzzle. "I'm glad you like to do these. I never can get the numbers right. Are you sure this is correct?"

He nodded. "It has to be. All the lines across and all those going down have the numbers one through nine in them. You know you're wrong when you get to a point that some line has two of the same numbers in it. Then you've made a mistake. I did this very carefully, and there are no mistakes showing up."

"I'm not questioning you, Alex, but I've been doing a lot of thinking since I received that call and the puzzles started coming. Something popped into my mind this morning, and I wanted to ask your opinion."

"Okay, what is it?"

She took a deep breath. "Do you think Mr. Mitchell died in the fall from the bridge?"

"Of course he did. Nobody could have survived that fall."

"How can you be sure? You never recovered a body."

Alex shook his head. "Don't try to make this more complicated than it is. With the currents like they are in the river, his body is downstream somewhere. It may never be found. What made you start thinking about this anyway?"

"I think it's odd that a man called so soon after the newscast. What if it was Mr. Mitchell and he's the one sending all the clues?"

"It wasn't Mitchell. Harbor patrol combed the water around the bridge and along the banks for hours. If he had surfaced and come ashore, they would have seen him. He didn't survive the fall." He walked to the door and opened it. "Now let's go see what this next clue is going to tell us."

She started to protest, but she pursed her lips and nodded. Although she might wish Mr. Mitchell had survived that fall, Alex was right. It seemed highly unlikely. With a sigh, she reached into the drawer of her desk and pulled her purse out. "Then let's go."

He glanced at his watch. "I didn't realize the time. Would you like some lunch first?"

"That sounds good. Where would you like to go?"

"A new barbecue place opened a few blocks from here. Why don't we give it a try?"

She placed her purse strap over her shoulder and smiled. "Like we did every other barbecue place in the city? I don't think you'd ever get tired of eating it."

Alex chuckled as he walked over and held the door open for her. "You got that right. I guess you know me well."

Grace glanced up as she walked past and smiled. "I guess I do."

She expected him to frown at the teasing tone of her voice, but he didn't. Instead, he gave a small nod. "You've always known me better than anyone else."

She looked away from him and took a deep breath. For the first time in the past few days she felt Alex was more relaxed around her than he had been before. Perhaps dinner at her home last night and her father's apology had been what he needed to see it was possible for them to be friends again. She hoped so, because she liked that he was more like the old Alex. She only hoped they could continue this comfortable truce.

Alex frowned as he pulled into the parking lot at the entrance to the Wolf River Greenway and glanced over at Grace. "Are you sure you're following the coordinates correctly?"

She nodded. "Yes. The next clue has to be hidden somewhere along the greenway."

He came to a stop in one of parking places and turned off the engine then turned toward her. "After what happened yesterday, there's no way we're going onto a path that runs through a forest and along the banks of the Wolf River. The guy who shot at us yesterday is probably out there somewhere waiting for us."

"I think you're right," she said. "What do you suggest we do?"

He pulled his cell phone out. "I'm going to call for some help. We can get some officers in there to search the forest. If they don't find anything, they can accompany us on the greenway when we go to find the spot. But we're not taking a step into that area before it's checked out first."

"That sounds good to me."

Alex made the call, and within minutes two

squad cars pulled into the parking lot. Alex stepped out of the car and met them. They listened as he explained the situation and then headed onto the path that led down to the river. He watched them go before he climbed back in the car with Grace.

"Aren't you going with them?" she asked.

"No. I don't want to leave you alone. That guy would probably love to find you all alone sitting in a car in a parking lot. It's better that I stay behind and make sure nothing happens to you."

She smiled. "Thanks, Alex."

"No need to thank me. I really am a good cop, Grace."

Her cheeks flushed, and she glanced down at her clenched fists in her lap. "I know that."

He pulled his gaze away from her to look out the window. "The temperature is dropping outside. If you get too cold, I can start the car and turn the heat on."

She shook her head and pulled her coat tighter around her. "There's no need for that. How long do you think they'll be?"

"I don't know. The length of the greenway at this point is over a mile long. They'll have to search through the forest all along the path. It could take a while."

She yawned. "Then I think I'll close my eyes for a few minutes. I didn't sleep well last night."

"Go ahead. I'll wake you when they get back."

She adjusted the seat to lean back and snuggled down in it. Within minutes a soft snore rippled from her throat. Alex sat still as long as he could before he opened the door and stepped out into the parking lot.

He glanced at his watch and wondered where the officers were at that moment and if they had found anything. Even if they didn't, he wasn't sure he and Grace should follow through with the search for another clue. Every time he thought about the bullets that had flown past their heads the day before, he felt a moment of fear. It was astonishing that neither of them had been injured.

So far he had helped Grace survive two attempts on her life. All it would take for the killer to succeed would be for him to let his guard down for one second. He had to make sure he didn't do that.

He began to pace up and down beside the car. Each time he passed the window, he looked inside at Grace who appeared to be sleeping as if she didn't have a care in the world. He wished he could feel that way, but the promise he'd made her father weighed heavily on his mind.

An hour later he was still pacing when the officers emerged from the greenway path. He stood still and waited as the officer in charge came toward him. "We didn't find anything, Detective. There wasn't a sign of anybody on the path or in the forest. We couldn't find any evidence that anyone had been there recently."

Alex breathed a sigh of relief. "That's good to know. As I told you, we have a note from a suspected killer. He claims he's left a clue for us in the woods. We need to find it, and I'd like for your men to accompany us in case he decides to show up while we're there."

The officer nodded. "We can do that."

Alex opened the car door, leaned in and shook Grace's shoulder. "Grace, wake up. The officers are back."

She bolted into a sitting position and wiped at her eyes. "Oh, I didn't mean to go to sleep. Did they find anything?"

"No, but they're going back with us. Are you ready?"

She nodded, stepped out of the car and pulled the GPS unit from her pocket. She looked around at the gathered officers and took a deep breath. "Well, let's go see what our friend has planned for us today."

Alex's heart thudded, and he fell into step

with her. The officers fanned out on either side of them and behind as they headed for the path. Alex pulled his gun from the holster and bit down on his lip. They would soon know what Grace's mysterious caller had in store for them today.

Grace consulted the GPS coordinates as she, Alex, and the officers stepped onto the paved path that meandered along the banks of the Wolf River. Since she'd been back in Memphis, she'd enjoyed many weekend afternoons walking the pathway. Today was different, and it wasn't just the December chill in the air. The police officers who provided protection for them were a reminder of the danger involved in what they were about to do.

Out of the corner of her eye, she noticed Alex's gaze sweeping back and forth across the path and into the forest. He held his gun as if he was ready to fire at a moment's notice. They walked in silence for a few minutes before Alex spoke. "This is my first time along the greenway. It must be nice out here in the spring."

She glanced at him, but he was staring past her into the trees. "You don't have to try and keep me calm, Alex. I know we're in a dangerous position out in the open like this."

His face flushed, and he glanced at her. "No, I'm serious. I've never been out here before."

She laughed, and the tension in her body eased a bit. "You need to get out more often. You don't know what you're missing. I love walking along this path and looking at the river and the trees and plants all around. It makes me feel good, knowing this is a protected green area where I can enjoy what God has put in the world for us. By the time this project is finished, this path we're on is going to stretch for thirty miles all the way downtown from Germantown and Collierville."

One of the officers walking beside her spoke up. "She's right. You should get out here this spring and enjoy some of the activities."

Grace looked over her shoulder at all the officers and smiled. "Maybe all of you can join me some Saturday for a short hike along this trail."

After she spoke the words, she tensed. How would Alex react to her invitation? Would he think she wasn't taking today's mission seriously enough? To her relief, he smiled.

"I hope the next time we're not after some crazy guy who wants to shoot us."

"Me, too." She glanced down at the GPS unit. "Maybe we'll catch him before then, and he'll be safely behind bars."

No one spoke again as they continued walking along the pathway. After about a mile Grace stopped and pointed to the trees alongside the paved walkway. "It's in there."

Alex's gaze drifted over the densely covered area. "I'm glad the leaves are off. Maybe it won't be too difficult to find whatever's been left. Let's see what it is."

The police fanned out in a circle, and they all walked into the woods. They'd only been searching for a few minutes when Grace spotted a manila envelope. It stuck out from underneath a large rock that had been placed at the base of a tree. "I think I have something."

The officers formed a protective ring around Grace and continued scanning the forest as Alex trudged through the undergrowth, stopped beside her and glanced down. "He didn't hide this very well, did he?"

"No. He wanted to make sure we found it. Since there aren't any other rocks that size around, he must have moved this one from down near the river." She took a deep breath. "Let's see what it is."

She picked up the bubble-cushioned mailer that looked to be about six by nine inches and ripped the seal open. Then she stuck her hand inside and pulled out an object wrapped in a piece of paper.

"What's that?" Alex asked.

"I don't know." Grace frowned and unwrapped the object. A carved wooden wolf lay inside. She picked up the carving and turned it over and over as she studied it. Suddenly she winced. "Ouch!"

Alex stepped closer. "What's the matter?"

She shook her head. "I'm okay. There's a sharp edge on the wolf, and it pricked my finger."

He frowned. "Does it hurt?"

"No, but it startled me." She turned the carving around in her hand again, careful not to touch the edge, and then glanced at the paper it had been wrapped in. She swallowed hard at the words on the page. "He's left me another note. It says, 'Some ancient people thought the wolf represented danger. Landon found out it did. Are you next?'"

Alex raked his hand through his hair. "Okay, that's it. This guy is getting too vocal in his threats. You are getting out of this investigation right now before it gets more dangerous."

Grace glanced down at the wolf and the note again. "Don't be ridiculous. We must be getting closer, or he wouldn't feel the need to voice these threats."

Alex shook his head and glanced around the area. "We don't know if he's out there in the trees watching us or not. He could have you in the sights of a rifle right now." He grabbed her by the arm and pulled her toward the pathway as he called out to the officers. "We're leaving. Let's get out of here now."

Propelled by Alex's grip on her arm, Grace stumbled forward as she stuck the note and the wolf in her coat pocket. Once on the pathway, Alex didn't slow down but kept a tight hold on her arm as they strode back toward the entrance. She glanced over her shoulder, and the officers hurried along the path behind them.

After about half a mile Grace winced at the numbing pain radiating through her trembling legs. What was Alex's hurry? Her chest heaved, and she panted for breath. "Alex, please slow down. You're walking too fast for me."

His gaze swept the pathway and the trees beside it. "We need to get out of here, Grace. There are too many places someone could be hiding. We'll slow down when we get to the parking lot."

She nodded and allowed him to pull her forward. By the time they'd gone five hundred feet farther her heart pounded so hard, she thought her chest might explode any minute. Her rubbery legs wanted to collapse, but she pushed on.

A sudden crushing pain gripped her chest, and she gasped for breath. A sound from somewhere in her head filled her, and she glanced toward the trees. She shook her head to clear away the dizziness and squinted at the image staring at her from between two trees. With every ounce of strength she could muster she pulled free of Alex. "Look who's here," she mumbled.

Alex jerked to a stop, whirled to face the trees, and pointed his gun in that direction. "Who is it?"

The other officers surrounded them within seconds. "What's going on?" she heard one say.

"Something's wrong with Grace," Alex said, but his voice seemed to be coming from far away.

She frowned at the gun in Alex's hand. There was no need for that. She glanced back at the familiar face in the trees staring at her, held out her hand and wiggled her fingers. "It's all right. You can come to me."

Alex turned back to her. "I don't see..." His eyebrows drew together as he scanned her face. "Grace, are you all right?"

"I'm fine." She looked up at Alex. "Why won't

he come here?" She closed her eyes as another wave of dizziness swept over her. She reached for Alex, and he caught her in his arms when she toppled toward him.

"Grace, what's the matter?" He knelt down and cradled her in his arms. "You're not making any sense. Who did you see?"

She raised a shaking finger and pointed to the trees. "Snowball. I'll ride him home."

"The pony you had when you were a child?" Alex turned his head to stare in the direction she pointed, then back to her. "Where is he?"

"Right there," she gasped. "Don't you see him?"

"There's nothing there, Grace."

What was the matter with Alex? Didn't he recognize the pony they'd ridden together when they were children? She struggled to push to her feet, but Alex's strong arms held her still. "He's there. I want to ride him."

Her eyesight blurred, and she blinked to clear her vision. When she reopened her eyes, the pony had disappeared. She frowned and glanced up at a strange man who hovered over her. Several other faces looked down at her. "Wh-who are you?" she stammered.

"Grace, it's Alex. Don't you recognize me?"

She shook her head and tried to pull from

this stranger's grasp. "Don't touch me," she screamed. "Alex, where are you?" she yelled.

"I'm right here, Grace."

She looked up into the face of the man who spoke, but she didn't know him. "Do you know Alex?"

"Grace, I'm Alex."

She saw his lips move, but the ringing in her ears drowned out his words. He leaned closer, and she tried to speak. Her breath hitched in her throat, and her words died on her lips.

The man moved slightly, and she saw a cell phone in his hand. With a sigh she surrendered to the darkness that crept over her.

Alex started to punch in 911 on his cell phone, but one of the other officers was already calling on his phone. Alex cradled Grace's limp body in his arms as another officer helped him to his feet. He glanced at the man on the phone. "Tell them to meet us at the parking lot. We're almost there."

He held her close as he ran down the path that led back to where he'd left his car. He heard the sirens just before he and the officers reached the entrance to the greenway and stumbled into the parking lot at the same moment the ambulance pulled to a stop.

The EMTs were out of the ambulance almost before they'd come to a stop, and Alex laid Grace on the gurney they pulled out. Alex stepped back and watched Grace's pale face as the two men began to check her vitals.

One of them glanced around at him. "Are you the officer who called this in?"

The man who'd called stepped forward. "No, I did."

The EMT turned his attention back to Alex. "Did anything unusual happen to cause her to faint?"

"No. We were on our way back to the parking lot when she collapsed. She started breathing heavily, and she became disoriented. She didn't recognize me and thought she saw a pony she had when she was a child."

The second EMT pulled the stethoscope he'd been using to check her heartbeat from his ears and glanced at his partner. "Heartbeat is weak and breathing is shallow. Let's get her on some oxygen and put her in the ambulance. We need to get to the E.R. right away."

Alex nodded. "I'll follow in my car." He turned to the officers who'd accompanied them on the greenway. "Thanks, guys. I appreciate all your help today. I need to go to the hospital."

The officer in charge nodded. "You go on.

I've never seen anything like what happened to her out there. Let us know how she gets along."

"I will."

He cast one last look at Grace before he ran back to his car. Within minutes he was headed up the street. The ambulance's siren and the wail of the one on his unmarked police car split the afternoon air. Traffic pulled out of their way and allowed them to speed unchecked along the street.

Alex roared into the hospital parking lot and jumped from his car as soon as it came to a stop. He knew from experience he wouldn't be allowed through the bay where the EMTs took Grace, so he paused in the parking lot long enough to call his office and alert his partners, Brad and Seth, to what had happened before he ran toward the doors of the emergency room waiting area.

He rushed inside, came to a stop at the desk and held up his badge. "The EMTs just brought my friend Grace Kincaid in. I followed the ambulance here."

The receptionist peered over the rim of her glasses, which sat propped on her nose. "I'll let you know when there's any news."

He opened his mouth to protest, but he realized it would do no good. As difficult as it was going to be, he had to wait until the doctor had determined what had happened to Grace. He groaned and slunk off to find a seat in the crowded room.

He'd barely settled in his chair before he thought of Grace's parents. He'd promised them he would keep their daughter safe and he hadn't. The bad thing was that he had no idea what had happened to her. Had their mysterious caller with his GPS puzzles been able to cause Grace's collapse?

"Alex." The sound of his name being call jerked him from his thoughts, and he found Laura Austin, his partner Brad's wife and Grace's best friend, standing in front of him. He jumped to his feet, and she threw her arms around him. "I just finished a counseling session upstairs, and Brad called to tell me Grace has been brought in."

He released her, and they sat down together on the couch. "I'm glad he did. I didn't know if you were working here or at Cornerstone Clinic today. Thank you for coming down."

Laura smiled. "Where else would I be? I've always been there when Grace has gotten into scrapes. But tell me what's happened. Brad said she's unconscious."

She listened as Alex related the events earlier

on the greenway. When he got to the part about how she had become delusional and passed out, his voice grew husky. He swallowed before finishing his story. "I've been over everything that happened on the greenway, but I can't figure out what caused her attack. It was like some allergic reaction."

Laura pursed her mouth and frowned. "Could it have been something in the environment? A tree or plant?"

"I thought of that, but it's December. There's very little vegetation out there."

Laura thought for a moment. "Then did she touch anything?"

Alex shook his head. "Nothing but the…" He stopped in midsentence, and his eyes widened. "The wood carving!"

His loud words startled Laura, and she jumped. "What are you talking about?"

"The envelope contained a carving of a wolf and a note. She touched those. The carving had a sharp edge on it, and she pricked her finger with it. That has to be it!" He sprang from his seat. "They're still in her pocket. I need to tell the doctor to test them."

He took a step to go to the desk, but Laura grabbed his arm to stop him. "Wait, Alex. You can't go back there, but as a nurse, I can. I'll go tell the doctor. You sit tight, and I'll let you know what he says."

He nodded. "All right, but tell the doctor to be careful. He needs to wear gloves before handling those items."

"I'll tell him and be right back." Laura strode across the room, stopped at the desk and spoke with the receptionist. She nodded and pushed a button, and the entrance to the treatment area opened.

Alex sat down and waited for Laura to return. It seemed like hours before he saw the door open again and Laura emerge. He was on his feet before she reached him. "How is she?"

"She's still unconscious."

"What did the doctor say when you told him about the note and the carving?"

"The doctor found both of them in Grace's pocket. He's sent them to the lab for testing. They should know something in a little while. In the meantime, we just have to wait."

He sank back on the couch and raised a shaking hand to wipe his forehead. "Waiting has always been hard for me to do, but I'm glad you're here."

She sighed, glanced at her watch and rose to her feet. "I wish I could stay, but I need to get back to work. I'll check with you later to see how Grace is doing. When she wakes up, tell her I was here."

He stood and gave her a kiss on the cheek. "Thanks for coming, Laura."

She smiled before she turned and walked down the hallway that led into the hospital proper. He stared after her for a moment and then stepped to the side of the room and pulled out his cell phone. There was no putting off the inevitable any longer. He had to call Grace's parents and tell them he hadn't been able to protect their daughter the way he'd promised.

SIX

Grace opened her eyes and frowned as she tried to determine where she was. She lay in a bed, but this wasn't the comfortable mattress she was so used to. She squinted at a small light shining through a cracked door that led into another room, a bathroom perhaps. A soft snore alerted her she wasn't alone, and she turned her head to look to her right.

In the darkened room she could make out the form of her mother in the chair next to the bed. She tried to raise her head, but it was no use. She slumped back, her head against the pillow and moaned.

Her mother jerked upright and was on her feet in one swift move. She leaned over the bed and gazed down at her. "Grace, are you awake?"

She licked at her dry lips and struggled to speak. "Wh-where am I?"

"You're in the hospital."

Grace closed her eyes and tried to remember

what had happened. The greenway popped into her mind, and her eyes blinked open. "Alex?"

Her mother patted her arm. "Alex is fine. You collapsed while the two of you were with the police officers at the greenway. They called 911 and got you here in time. You're going to be fine."

A memory of running along the path returned, but nothing else. "Wh-where is Alex?"

"He called us after you were brought in, and your father and I came right away. When the doctors told us you were going to be all right, Alex took your father home so I could stay. He'll be by in the morning to see you."

She nodded and closed her eyes. She wanted to talk more, but she couldn't concentrate. Right now she wanted to go back to sleep. There would be time later to find out why she was in the hospital.

The next time Grace opened her eyes, the sun streamed through the windows. She turned her head toward where her mother had sat the last time she awoke and saw instead Alex reading a newspaper in a chair next to her bed.

He glanced up and saw her looking at him. "Good morning. So you're finally awake. I thought you were going to sleep all day."

She frowned. "What time is it?"

"It's nearly ten o'clock."

"Why aren't you at work?"

"I'll go in after lunch. I wanted to be with you when you woke up."

She looked around the room. "Where's my mother? She was here when I woke up before."

"I sent her home when I got here. She hadn't slept any, and I told her I'd stay with you."

"What about my father? Mother told me you took him home last night."

Alex nodded. "He didn't want to leave, but he was really tired. I took him home and got him settled in bed."

Grace's eyes grew wide. "You helped my father to bed?"

Alex's face flushed, and he nodded. "I was glad to do it. Your mother wanted to stay here, and I told her I'd make sure your father got to bed."

"Thank you for doing that." A sudden thought struck her. "But it was the maid's night off. Did he stay in the house alone?"

Alex shook his head. "No. I couldn't leave him alone. I stayed in the guest room and put the phone by his bed so he could call my cell phone during the night if he needed me."

Grace's mouth gaped open. "You stayed at our house with my father?"

"I did."

Tears filled Grace's eyes. "Thank you, Alex. That was very kind of you. Especially since you and my father haven't had a good relationship in the past."

Alex smiled at her. "When your father apologized, I knew I had to meet him halfway if we were ever to overcome the memories of the past. The more I'm around him, the more I can see his good qualities. I think we may end up being friends."

Grace smiled, too, and wiped at the corner of her eye. "Nothing would make me happier."

Alex cleared his throat and folded the newspaper he'd been holding when she woke up. "Laura's been here several times. She came in yesterday after we got here, and she dropped by this morning on her way to work."

"I hope she wasn't worried about me."

His eyes darkened, and his gaze lingered on her face. "We were all worried about you, Grace."

She tried to pull her gaze away from him, but she couldn't. "I'll call her later." Alex stared at her without speaking, and after a moment Grace cleared her throat and started to rise. "I need to get up."

Alex jumped to his feet and shook his head.

"You can't get up until a nurse comes to help you. I'll call for one."

He grabbed the cord for the call button and punched it. "She's awake," he responded when the nurse's station answered.

Within seconds a nurse entered the room, stopped beside the bed and smiled. "It's good to see you awake. How are you feeling?"

Grace hesitated before she answered. "I'm not sure yet."

"Do you think you're strong enough to walk to the bathroom?"

"I think so."

The nurse turned to Alex. "If you'll excuse us for a moment, I'll help Miss Kincaid get freshened up a bit. I'll call you back in when we have her ready for breakfast."

Alex nodded. "I'll be outside."

When he'd exited the room, the nurse released the side rails of the bed and supported Grace as she sat up on the side of the bed. "How's that?"

A wave of dizziness swept over her, and she swayed. "I'll be okay in a moment."

"Take it easy. You've been through a lot."

Grace looked up at her and frowned. "What happened to me?"

"We can talk about that after you're feeling stronger. First, let's get you ready to visit with that handsome police detective. From what the other nurses tell me, he was a nervous wreck when you were brought in. He paced the waiting room floor for hours. It's plain to see how he feels about you."

Grace smiled and shook her head. "We're really good friends. We have been since we were children."

The nurse arched her eyebrows. "All I can say is I wish I had a friend who cared about me so much."

Grace laughed and allowed herself to be helped to her feet. Thirty minutes later with a clean hospital gown on and her breakfast tray in front of her Grace sat up in bed and smiled as Alex walked back into the room.

"I was beginning to wonder where you'd gone."

He grinned and slipped his cell phone in his pocket. "I was on the phone with Brad. He said Laura is worried sick about you."

Grace laid her fork on the tray and looked at Alex as he sat down in the chair next to the bed. "I've been trying to remember what happened. The last thing I remember is you pulling me along the path. I thought my lungs were going to explode. What happened?"

"You collapsed, and we called 911."

"I know that, but why did I faint?"

Alex shifted to the edge of his chair and stared at her. "Do you remember the wolf and the note?"

"Yes."

"And do you remember pricking your finger on a sharp edge?"

"Yes."

Alex inhaled a deep breath. "When the lab tested the wolf and the note, they found both of them were covered with cyanide. The poison was able to enter your system through the small nick on your finger, and your mysterious puzzle maker knew that's what would happen. If we hadn't gotten here in time, you might be dead now."

"Cyanide?" A shiver ran up her spine, and Grace flinched. "But I thought cyanide killed you right away."

"From what the doctor said, that only happens in the movies. It actually works much slower than chomping down on a capsule and dying instantly."

"Was I really in danger of dying?"

"You could have. The doctor told us cyanide poisoning can occur in different ways—by eating cyanide-laced food, inhaling cyanide gas or absorbing it through the skin. I wrote down what they gave you as an antidote." He pulled a piece of paper out of his pocket and glanced down at it. "They gave you sodium nitrite and sodium thiosulfate. You'll be fine in a few days. You just need to rest."

Grace rubbed her hand over her forehead. "I wish I could remember. I recall trying to keep up with you on the pathway, and I remember falling down. But nothing else." She glanced up at Alex. "Did I just faint?"

He fidgeted in his chair. "I thought you were conscious, but you were talking out of your head."

"What did I say?"

"You said you saw Snowball standing in the forest."

Her eyes grew wide. "Snowball? I thought I saw my pony?"

He chuckled. "Yeah. You said you wanted to ride him home."

"Did I say anything else?"

He hesitated a moment, then took a deep breath. "No, you lost consciousness. None of us could figure out what happened to you. It was really scary, Grace. Thank goodness we got you here in time."

"I remember being dizzy, and then I felt really

frightened." She swallowed the fear that rose in her throat. "Alex, he's tried to kill me twice."

He looked at her without blinking. "I know. This has gotten out of hand, Grace. We can't let this happen again. He might be successful the next time."

"But what are we going to do? We can't let him scare us off."

He shook his head. "I don't know. I haven't figured it out yet, but I will. I've promised your parents I'll keep you safe, and I intend to keep that promise. For now, though, you need to rest and get well."

"You're right. I should have listened to you all along. Right now I'm so grateful to be alive, and I have you to thank for that. You've done what you promised."

He leaned over and covered her hand with his. "Don't worry, Grace. We're going to get this guy. We just have to go about it in a different way now."

She nodded and lay back on her pillow. Her heartbeat quickened at the thought of what might have happened if Alex and the other officers hadn't been with her yesterday. For some reason the person who had killed Landon had set his sights on her. She'd been fortunate to escape him twice, but she might not be able to a third time.

Perhaps she'd been wrong to push Alex into including her in this investigation. Now she had put him in the position of not only finding a killer but protecting her at the same time. Her stubborn determination to have her way in this investigation had put him in danger also, and she regretted that. She should have realized he was the trained police officer and listened to him, but she had pushed him into including her. And he had given in, just like he always had when they were children.

She glanced over at him sitting beside the bed. "I'm sorry, Alex."

He lowered the newspaper he was reading. "For what?"

"For insisting on being included in this investigation. I have put you in danger, and I'm truly sorry for that."

His Adam's apple bobbed up and down, and after a moment he spoke. "It's something I face every day, Grace. It's not your fault that somebody wants to kill you. I just want to keep you safe."

Tears filled her eyes, and she blinked. "Thank you. I know you'll do that."

She looked down at her hand on top of the blanket and stared at Landon's ring on her finger. Whoever had tried to kill her had kept that ring for twelve years. How she wished it could talk and tell her where it had been, but that was impossible. After a moment she turned over, pulled the covers up to her chin and closed her eyes. She needed to sleep. Maybe when she woke she wouldn't be haunted by the thought of someone lurking in the shadows and planning his next attempt on her life.

Alex drank the last drops out of the soda can, tossed it into the waiting room trash can and glanced at his watch. The doctor had been in Grace's room for about fifteen minutes. What could be taking him so long?

Alex walked to the door and peered down the hall toward Grace's room. A nurse stepped out and walked back toward the nurse's station. He stopped her when she drew even with him. "Excuse me, but is the doctor still in Miss Kincaid's room?"

She nodded. "He is, but he'll be out in a few minutes."

"Thank you." He smiled at her and watched as she continued to her destination. He was about to go back and sit down when his cell phone rang. Brad's number flashed on caller ID. He raised the phone to his ear. "Hey, Brad. What's up?"

"I thought you were coming to the office this afternoon."

Alex sighed and rubbed the back of his neck. "I had intended to, but I kept waiting for the doctor. I wanted to hear what he would say about Grace's condition."

"Has he come yet?"

"Yeah, he's in with her now. I'm waiting for him to leave. Then I'll probably come in."

"No need to, buddy. Everything's under control here. Stay with Grace as long as she needs you. I know it's hard for her parents to be there with her father's condition."

"He was here for a while last night, but I took him home."

Brad's startled gasp vibrated in Alex's ear. "Since when did you and Harrison Kincaid get so friendly? I thought the guy hated you."

Alex chuckled. "Not anymore. It seems the shooting has made a changed man out of him. He's turned his life over to God. In fact, he asked me to forgive him for the way he treated me when I was growing up."

"I never thought I'd hear that, but I'm glad he's changed. It's too bad it took him being shot to open his eyes to God's love for him."

"I guess you're right."

"When you see Grace, tell her Laura is coming back to the hospital when she gets off work. She wanted to stay this morning, but she had to get to work because they were short staffed at the clinic. She has some counseling sessions later at the hospital, so she's going to see Grace before her patients get there."

"I told her Laura had come by, so she's looking forward to seeing her."

"Well, they have been best friends since elementary school." Brad hesitated a moment. "Are things getting better between you and Grace?"

Alex sighed. "I think we're getting there. It's better than it has been."

"Good. Laura and I hate to think about our two best friends at odds with each other. We're praying you and Grace can learn to at least be civil to each other."

"Thanks, Brad."

"Now if Laura had her way…" He paused for a moment. "Hey, I'm getting a call on another line. I'll check with you later."

Alex ended the call and stared at his phone for a moment. Brad didn't have to finish his sentence for him to know what he was about to say. Brad and Laura would be happy if he and Grace could get together again. They were his closest friends, too, but he couldn't make them understand it was too late for him and Grace. She had chosen another life instead of having one with him, and he was doing all right on his own.

Gritting his teeth, Alex whirled and stormed back into the waiting room. He strode toward the window, stopped in front of it and looked out at the parking lot. Snow had begun to fall, and he watched the swirling flakes fall to the ground.

Maybe they were going to have a white Christmas this year. When he and Grace were children, they'd wish every year that it would snow for the holidays, but Memphis had seen little snowfall during their childhood. The biggest one had been when they were ten years old. They'd built a snowman and placed one of her father's hats on its head. He smiled at the memory. Why did things like that keep popping into his head?

Before he could answer the question in his mind, he heard footsteps in the hall, and he turned to see the doctor walk past the waiting room. He needed to find out what the doctor had said. He strode down the hall to Grace's room and knocked before entering.

"Come in," she called out.

Her bed was positioned so that she was sitting upright, and she smiled when he walked in. His heart thudded at the thought that she'd almost died the day before. Having her back in his life might be difficult, but having her dead would be unbearable.

He returned the smile and sat down beside the bed. "What did the doctor say?"

"He wants me to stay another night, but he feels sure I can go home tomorrow."

Alex nodded. "I think that's wise."

"I also talked to my boss at the station. I have two weeks of vacation coming, and I'm going to take off until after Christmas. That should give us some time to figure out where we go from here in the investigation of Landon's death."

His eyes grew wide, and he jumped to his feet. "Whoa, there. What makes you think we go anywhere after what's happened?"

She sat up straighter and clenched her hands in her lap. "Because we haven't found the answer yet." She took a deep breath. "I've thought about this since I woke up. I have to admit I'm scared this guy will come after me again. I don't think I should go looking for any more of his clues, but we can't just drop the investigation."

Alex shook his head. "No, Grace. You've had two attempts on your life. You need to stay out of this. Let me handle it by myself."

"I know you're the trained police officer, and I'm just a nosy news reporter. But I can't give up." She held up her hand. "Look at that ring, Alex. Somebody killed Landon and kept it for twelve years. I want to know who did that. Please don't shut me out. Let me help you with this case. I promise I'll do whatever you say."

He ran his hand through his hair and muttered under his breath. "Why are you so pigheaded? I'm only trying to protect you. I was scared to death yesterday that you were going to die before I could get help. I don't want to go through that again."

Tears pooled in her eyes, and she nodded. "I'm sorry you were scared, but I'm so thankful you were there. Please, Alex, help me find out the truth, and then I'll never ask you for anything again."

He looked at her for a moment, and he felt his resolve crumbling. He sighed in resignation. "Okay, but no more puzzles. This time we're doing it my way. We'll investigate with some good old-fashioned police work. Do you understand?"

She nodded, and the smile that lit her face sent a warm rush through his veins. "Yes, and I promise I'll listen to you."

His gaze drifted over her face, and his breath hitched in his throat when he spied the tiny scar at the edge of her hairline on the right side of her forehead. He reached over and let his finger trace the jagged line that had faded with time. "You'll listen to me like you did when I was teaching you to ride the bicycle you got for Christmas?"

She reached up, placed her finger on top of his, and looked into his eyes. "It wasn't your fault I had a wreck and cut my head. I should have listened to you and let you hold on to me until I learned to balance better."

"But your father blamed me, and I blamed myself, too."

"I never wanted you to do that." She smiled. "This scar is very special to me. Every time I look in the mirror to comb my hair, I see it and I think of you. It's helped me get through a lot of difficult times."

He pulled away from her, and she smiled. Then without saying another word, she lay back in bed and closed her eyes. He sat down in the chair beside her bed and picked up a magazine that lay on the bedside table. After a few minutes her breathing became steady, and he realized she had dropped off to sleep.

There was work to be done at the police station, but he couldn't bring himself to leave. He'd made a promise to her father that he would protect her, and he would do whatever it took to keep that promise. In the past three days she'd almost been killed twice, and he couldn't let that happen again. If their puzzle maker was determined to get to Grace, he was going to have to go through him first.

SEVEN

Grace closed the high school annual she'd been looking at for the past hour, laid it on the den desk and glanced at her watch. This was her second day home from the hospital, and she'd been waiting for Alex to visit all morning. Now that it was midafternoon, she'd begun to wonder if he was coming at all.

He'd brought her home yesterday and had barely seen her settled before he rushed off to his office. But she really couldn't blame him. For the past few days he'd been at the hospital a good deal of the time, and his work had probably piled up while he'd been away.

She stood, walked to the window and pulled back the curtain. The snow that had fallen while she was in the hospital had melted, but the weather prediction called for more accumulation before Christmas, which was only a week and a half away.

The sound of someone entering the room

caught her attention, and she turned to see Alex coming toward her. Tired lines creased his face, and his eyes looked as if he hadn't slept in days. She frowned. "I didn't hear you come in."

"Nancy let me in."

She took a step toward him. "You look tired. Are you all right?"

A small smile pulled at his lips, and he nodded. "It's been a hard day at work. My partner Seth and I have been working on a case with a retired police officer for a while now, and it seems to be going nowhere. Besides I haven't slept much the past few nights."

"Why not?"

"For one thing I've been trying to figure out where we go with the Mitchell case now, and the other problem is my father."

Grace's eyebrows knit. "What's wrong with your father?"

He looked down at his feet, and she recognized the mannerism he'd had ever since they were children. She knew he would take a breath, look up in a few seconds and proceed to tell her something she probably didn't want to hear. She braced herself for what he was about to say. "Since my father retired to Florida, he's been after me to come down there. The town where he lives is going to hire a new police chief, and he wants me to apply for the job. He's been calling me every day about it."

Grace couldn't control the gasp that escaped her throat. It was as if someone had thrown a glass of ice water in her face. "You aren't seriously considering it, are you?"

Alex shrugged. "You know how I feel about Memphis, but my father's getting older and he's not well. I suppose I'm kind of in the same situation you were when you had to come back to Memphis because of your father's situation. Of course my dad's illness doesn't compare to what your father's going through, but he's my father. He needs me."

"I can understand that. Our parents took care of us when we were little. Now it seems it's our turn to help them. I'll be praying for you to make the right decision. When do you think you'll decide?"

"I told him I'd let him know at Christmas. He's coming here to spend it with me."

Grace smiled. "Then maybe I'll get to see him. I would like that."

Alex nodded. "Maybe so."

Grace took a deep breath and walked back to the desk where she'd placed the annuals she'd been studying before Alex arrived. She picked up one and opened it. "I found something I wanted to show you."

"What is it?" He walked over and peered down at the book she held.

She pointed to the three books on the desk and the one she held. "These are our high school annuals. I've been looking through them, and I've noticed something. In all the pictures of Landon in our freshman and sophomore years he looks like a happy boy. He's healthy-looking, and he's smiling in every picture. There are some action shots of him on the football field, and he's in a lot of pictures with groups of kids. He was one of the leaders in our geocache club during our sophomore year."

Alex nodded. "I remember how quick he was on the football field. Once he got started running toward the goal line, there was no stopping him. He was tough, and he could outrun anybody on the team. Coach thought Landon would get a scholarship to a major university."

Grace sank down in the desk chair and motioned for Alex to sit in the one beside her. "He had everything going for him. I don't understand what happened during our junior year that made his life start to fall apart."

She opened the annual from their junior year and pointed to his picture. "Look at his face. He had this cocky expression that he never had before. That's about the time he began to act like he was big man on campus. By the time we were seniors, he'd dropped out of the geocache club. He said he didn't have time for childish activities. He was into other things."

"Did he say what those other things were?"

Grace shook her head. "When I would ask, he'd just laugh and tell me I was better off not knowing. He dropped all his old friends, including me, quit the football team and took up with a whole new group of kids."

"I remember him quitting. Coach was fit to be tied, but Landon wouldn't change his mind. Do you know who his new friends were?"

"Yes. They were Jeremy Baker, Billy Warren, Sam Jefferson, Clay Mercer and Dustin Shelton."

Alex narrowed his eyes as if he was in deep thought. After a few moments, he nodded. "I remember them. They were a bunch of spoiled rich boys who drove the fastest cars and thought the rules didn't apply to them. Do you know where they are now?"

Grace grinned and laid the book on the desk. "No, but I know how we can find out."

"How?"

"I called our high school this morning and

talked with the secretary. Did you know that Mr. Donner is still the principal there?"

He nodded. "Yeah, I see his name in the paper from time to time when the school makes the news."

"Well, we have an appointment to see him in…" She paused and glanced at her watch. "In about thirty minutes. I'm glad I thought about calling this morning. This is the last day before Christmas break, and the school will be closed for the next two and a half weeks."

"Do you think he might know where these guys are now?" Alex asked.

Grace rolled her eyes and groaned. "I can't imagine his not knowing. There probably isn't a school in the whole state that has an alumni association as active as the one at our old school. I suppose that's to be expected since it's a private school that receives a lot of their operating funds from donations. Mr. Donner has even hired an office worker who makes it a priority to keep an updated address list of former students and their families. They send out newsletters and requests for contributions to the school all the time." She paused and propped her hands on her hips. "Sometimes it seems like I get two letters a week wanting me to donate to some program at the school."

Alex chuckled and nodded. "Yeah, I get them, too. In fact, I mailed a check last week for the fund-raiser for some new computers in the technology department."

"I got that letter, too."

Alex glanced at his watch. "Well, if we're going, we need to be on our way. Traffic may be heavy this time of day."

"My coat's in the hall closet. I'll get it."

He nodded and followed her from the room. When they reached the closet, she pulled the coat out, and he held it for her to slip her arms inside. Then he turned her to face him and pulled the coat tight around her. "It's cold outside today."

His fingers brushed her throat, and her pulse raced. "I know."

He stared at her for a moment, and his Adam's apple bobbed. Then he stepped back, cleared his throat and glanced over his shoulder. "Where are your parents?"

"They're upstairs. My father is taking a nap, and my mother is wrapping Christmas presents. She wants to get all of them under the tree tonight. And that reminds me, they said they'd like for you to stay for dinner."

He shook his head. "That's not necessary. I've already eaten here once this week."

She stopped and looked up at him. "It's an

invitation, Alex. They appreciate what you did for us."

"I didn't do anything special."

"You called for an ambulance and carried me from the greenway, then you brought my father home and put him to bed. You also stayed the night so he wouldn't be alone. You did a lot."

"It was no more than any friend would have done."

"Then stay and let us show you how much we appreciate your friendship."

He seemed to consider the offer, and she held her breath, waiting for his answer. After a moment he nodded. "Okay, I'll stay for dinner."

Grace smiled and opened the door. "Good. Now let's go see if our former principal can help us locate Landon's friends. If we can find them, they may be able to answer a lot of questions about what made Landon change from the boy we'd known and why he had a wolf's head tattooed on his shoulder."

The school had changed very little since the last time Alex had been inside. The trophy case still hung on the wall in the spot where it had been when he was a student, and posters of club meetings and extracurricular activities dotted the walls.

He stopped in front of the trophy case and saw the gold-plated championship cup his football team had won his senior year. The memory of the night they became state champs still excited him after all these years. He knew the coach had retired some years ago, but he had no idea where most of his teammates were. He hadn't kept up with anyone after high school except Grace and Brad.

The door to the school office opened, and Grace stepped out into the hall. She walked over and stopped beside him. "The principal is on the phone. His secretary will call us when he's ready to see us." She didn't speak for a few minutes as she looked at the awards inside the case. "There's the state championship trophy from our senior year. Do you remember the night of the game?"

He straightened and grinned. "Yeah, I do. I couldn't believe we beat the top-ranked school, but we did. We all went to that hamburger place down the street to celebrate."

She laughed. "I was so proud of you because you'd been named Most Valuable Player for the game, but you shrugged it off like it was no big deal."

He grinned. "I thought it was more macho to pretend I didn't care. Of course I was proud."

He looked at the trophy again. "Seeing it after all this time takes me back to our school days. I can't believe it's been twelve years since we graduated from high school."

She rolled her eyes. "I can. A lot has happened since then. I'm twelve years older, and I know I'm not that young girl anymore. I check the mirror every morning to see how many new wrinkles I have."

Alex laughed and cocked an eyebrow. "I don't think you have anything to worry about. You're prettier now than you were then."

She batted her eyelashes at him. "Thank you, kind sir. I needed that, especially after spending two days in the hospital."

The teasing tone of her voice made him smile. He was about to reply when the office door opened, and the secretary stuck her head out. "Mr. Donner is off the phone now. He said for you to come in."

They followed the young woman inside and to the door of Mr. Donner's private office. When he saw them, he rose from behind his desk and motioned for them to enter. "Grace Kincaid and Alex Crowne. It's good to see you."

"And you, too," Alex said as he reached out and shook the principal's hand. "Thank you for seeing us on such short notice."

He shook Grace's hand and motioned for them to take two chairs in front of his desk. "How long has it been since you graduated? Eight years?"

Grace chuckled. "No, twelve."

Mr. Donner shook his head. "It can't have been that long. It seems like yesterday."

Alex settled back in his chair and let his gaze travel over the room. He smiled when he spied a framed picture on a shelf behind the principal's desk. It was a younger Mr. Donner standing in the parking lot beside a motorcycle he used to ride to school. He laughed and pointed to the picture. "I remember the day that was taken. Some of the guys on the football team were examining your bike when you came outside to go home. You asked one of the fellows to take your picture."

Mr. Donner smiled. "Yeah, I was proud of that bike."

Alex nodded. "We could tell. We thought it was really cool that our principal rode a motorcycle. Do you still ride?"

"I do. Not that bike of course. I gave it to my son when he got older and bought myself a bigger one. I ride in a club with a bunch of friends. It's my only hobby." He clasped his hands on top of his desk and leaned forward. "But I doubt if you came by to talk to me about my bike. Tell me what brings you back to school."

Alex cast one last glance at the picture before he looked back at Mr. Donner. "I don't know if you've heard or not, but I'm with the Memphis Police Department. I work on cold cases, and at present I'm investigating the death of Landon Mitchell who was thought to have committed suicide the year Grace and I were seniors."

Mr. Donner sat back, rested his elbows on the chair arms and tented his fingers in front of him. "I remember when that happened. It was a horrible thing." He glanced at Grace. "I saw your coverage about Landon's father and heard you say you would be trying to find out the truth. Are the two of you working together?"

Grace nodded. "We are."

Mr. Donner pursed his mouth as if in deep thought before he spoke. "I've always had my doubts about Landon's death. I thought the police ruled it a suicide too quickly. Have they reopened the case?"

"It was never officially closed even though they did recover his body and do an autopsy. The investigators thought it was suicide but the medical examiner couldn't make a definite ruling because of other injuries to the body, such as a head wound."

Mr. Donner frowned. "But couldn't that have been caused by the impact from the fall?"

"That's the problem," Alex said. "It might have been, and it might not have been. I hope this time we find the answer."

"What can I do to help?"

Alex settled back in his chair and took a deep breath. "If you heard Grace's report about Mr. Mitchell's death, then you know he thought his son was involved in some secret society here at the school and that they killed him. Have you ever suspected there might be a club that operates in the shadows out of the administration's sight?"

Mr. Donner thought for a moment before he shook his head. "Soon after I took this job, I heard rumors of such a group. I investigated it and never found anything that would make me think such a group existed."

Alex pursed his lips and thought about what the principal had said for a moment. "Would it surprise you to know such a group was talked about often in the locker room?"

The man's eyes grew wide and he nodded. "Really? I talked to students I knew to be trustworthy, and they all assured me no such group existed."

"It could have just been kids talking without any real knowledge of a secret society." He glanced at Grace. "But it's still difficult to understand why Landon would suddenly drop all his old friends and associate himself with a new group."

"Did he do that?" Mr. Donner asked.

Alex glanced at Grace. "Tell him about Landon's friends."

She scooted to the edge of her chair. "Landon and I dated up until our senior year when he suddenly broke up with me. He also dropped all his old friends and started hanging out with a new group. I lost track of them after high school, and we wondered if you had any information on where they are now."

"I try to keep up with our graduates for our alumni council." He turned to his computer. "Give me a name, and I'll look him up."

"The first one is Sam Jefferson," Grace said.

Mr. Donner smiled. "I don't have to look him up. Sam is a lawyer with offices downtown. He's done really well for himself. In fact, my wife and I have used him when we've needed legal advice."

Alex pulled a small notepad from his pocket and wrote down Sam's information. "That's good to hear. What about Dustin Shelton?"

Mr. Donner sat back in his chair, a sad expression on his face. "I don't have to look him up, either. Dustin disappeared while on a trip to the Gulf Coast a few years after he graduated. I attended the memorial service his family had."

Alex relaxed his grip on the pen poised to write Dustin's address and stared at Mr. Donner. "I remember Dustin. He was in one of my classes. I'm sorry to hear that."

"Yes, it was very sad. His family has never recovered from not finding his body." He shifted in his chair. "Who's the next one, Grace?"

"Jeremy Baker."

"Um, I don't remember him, but I'm sure he's in the alumni database." He typed the name into the computer, and his eyebrows rose as the information came on the screen. "This is a coincidence."

Alex leaned forward. "What is?"

Mr. Donner looked up from the computer screen. "Jeremy died in California about five years ago." His forehead wrinkled, and he looked back to the screen. Suddenly he nodded. "I do remember something about this young man. I remember some of the teachers talking about a former student who was found shot to death in his apartment in California. The police thought he'd been killed in a home invasion."

Alex and Grace exchanged startled glances

before he wrote the latest information down. Then he swallowed and turned back to Mr. Donner. "What about Clay Mercer?"

He smiled. "Oh, I see Clay from time to time, although he lives in Nashville now. He's a political advisor and works with the governor's office."

Alex scribbled on the notepad and nodded. "What about Billy Warren?"

"Billy Warren," Mr. Donner murmured as he typed in the name. "Here he is. Oh, no. He's dead also. He was killed in a car wreck in Colorado four years ago." He glanced from Alex to Grace. "Those were the boys Landon had started hanging out with?"

"Yes." Alex's stomach roiled from the thoughts racing through his head. Of the six boys who had been friends, four of them were dead. The odds against that happening must be astronomical. He closed the notepad and glanced back at Mr. Donner. "We really appreciate your time today, but I know you're ready to begin your Christmas vacation. We won't take up any more of your time. It's been great being back here."

The principal stood and held out his hand. "Don't you two stay away so long before you come back to visit. If I can help you any more, please let me know."

Alex shook his hand and then Grace stood and did the same. "Thanks, Mr. Donner. It's been great seeing you today."

"It's always good to see you, Grace. And by the way, you know our annual fund-raiser is coming up in February. It would be great if you could maybe play it up on your newscast after Christmas. Let your viewers know the school you attended needs the support of the community if we are to continue providing quality programs to our students."

Grace smiled. "I'll see what I can do, Mr. Donner."

She turned toward the door, and Alex followed her from the room. They were almost to the front door of the school when a voice rang out in the hallway. "Grace Kincaid! What are you doing here?"

They whirled to face the man coming toward them. "Mr. Caldwell!" Grace hurried to him, and he enveloped her in a big hug. She pulled back and studied him at arm's length. "It's so good to see you. I haven't seen you in years."

Alex walked to where the two stood and stuck out his hand. "Mr. Caldwell, I don't know whether you remember me or not. I'm Alex Crowne."

The man grabbed Alex's hand and pumped it up and down. "Of course I remember. Who could forget that winning touchdown pass you threw in the state championship your senior year?" He leaned closer to Grace conspiratorially and said in a loud whisper, "We haven't won a title since then."

Grace laughed and looped her arm through Mr. Caldwell's. "Alex, this is my favorite teacher from my high school years. This man turned me on to writing and made me want to be a journalist. I owe him so much."

Mr. Caldwell gazed down at her and patted her hand. "You owe me nothing. It was a pleasure to teach a student who hung on my every word. I worried all the time that I would give out some wrong information in class and you would correct me."

Grace shook her head. "I wouldn't have known if you had. I was too busy trying to be the perfect student in your class."

He nodded and glanced at Alex. "I don't think I ever had you in my class, Alex."

"No, I was sorry I never got you for a teacher. Grace talked about you all the time. I guess you knew Landon Mitchell well, too, since he was your student."

"I did."

"And he was a good student?"

"He…" Mr. Caldwell hesitated. "He was a good student until about halfway through his junior year. Then something happened to him. It was like he didn't have his mind on his studies, and his grades took a nosedive. I talked to him and to his father, but nothing I said helped. By the middle of his senior year, I was afraid he might not graduate."

"I know," Grace said. "I saw it happening, too, but I couldn't figure it out. Did you have any theories concerning this abrupt change in him?"

Mr. Caldwell looked over his shoulder as if to make sure no one could hear what he was about to say. Then he leaned closer. "Of course the first thing you think about is drugs. He had all the symptoms of drug use—failing grades, avoiding old friends, skipping school, getting in trouble all the time. And then I heard he was involved with some secret group here at the school."

Alex's eyes grew wide. "What secret group?"

"I don't know who was in the group, but some of the kids told me they all had wolves tattooed on their shoulders. I was afraid they were selling drugs, but Mr. Donner wouldn't listen to me."

Alex and Grace exchanged quick glances. "Did you tell Mr. Donner about what the kids were saying?"

"Yes, but he dismissed it and wouldn't investigate. When I told him, he looked at me, laughed and said, 'Patrick, don't be ridiculous. There are no drugs in this school.' He doesn't want the school board to think there are any problems in this school, and he tries to keep quiet anything that might blemish the school's reputation and cut down on donations from alumni. He's been this way ever since he came here."

"So he buries his head in the sand and hopes things will work out?" Grace asked.

Mr. Caldwell nodded. "Yes. If he had taken my concerns seriously and allowed me to find out more, we might have prevented the problem we have now."

"And what kind of problem is that?" Alex asked.

"Drugs. Drugs are everywhere in this school, and the problem gets worse every day. The administration refuses to acknowledge it, and teachers can't fight it on their own. I'm thinking of retiring at the end of this year. I've already cut back to part-time, but I know it's time for me to do something else."

Grace's forehead wrinkled, and she grabbed Mr. Caldwell's arm. "What will you do?"

He shook his head. "I don't know, but I can't take much more of the atmosphere around here."

"I'm so sorry," Grace said. "The students are losing a great teacher."

Mr. Caldwell straightened to his full height. "My time here is drawing to a close. Somebody else is going to have to take up the fight." He glanced at his watch. "Oh, my. I didn't realize it's so late. I have some Christmas gifts to pick up on my way home. They're for some of the residents at a retirement home where I volunteer."

"That's a very nice thing for you to do," Grace said.

He shrugged and smiled. "I have no family, and neither do some of them. So we've become each other's family. I'll spend Christmas with them."

Grace grasped his hand once more. "You're a good man, Mr. Caldwell. It was great to see you again."

He smiled and took her hand with both of his. "It was good seeing you, Grace. Don't stay away so long again."

"I won't, and I hope you and your friends at the retirement home have a merry Christmas."

"I'm sure we will, and merry Christmas to both of you." Mr. Caldwell turned and hurried down the hall to the door that led to the faculty parking lot. When he exited, Grace turned to Alex. "Mr. Caldwell always seemed so sad when I was in his class. He talked about having no wife or children and how teaching was his life. Volunteering at a retirement home helps fill that void I suppose."

"I guess so," Alex replied.

She tilted her head and looked at him. "But his story is a bit different from Mr. Donner's. I wonder why the principal lied to us about never having heard about a secret group."

Alex pursed his lips and stared in the direction of the office. "I don't know, but he did give us some new information about Landon's friends. I think our next step should be to question Sam Jefferson. I'll call his office in the morning and get an appointment for us to see him. For now, let's go see what they're serving at the Kincaid house for dinner tonight."

"It sounds like you're becoming more comfortable being around my family. I'm glad. I've wanted that for years."

Alex didn't say anything as she headed toward

the door. Was he becoming more comfortable with her family? If he was, he needed to be careful. His experience with the Kincaids had only brought him heartache in the past, and it could happen again.

As much as he loved Memphis, maybe his father was right. That job in Florida might be just what he needed to start a new life. Just he and his father living where there was no cold weather and you could walk on the beach every day of the year. The more he thought about it, the more it appealed to him.

EIGHT

The minute she and Alex walked through the door at the law offices of Jefferson, Brooks and Dunbar the next morning Grace knew their old schoolmate Sam had done all right for himself. The waiting area resonated with the unspoken message one needed a fat bank account to afford this firm's high retainers and huge billing hours.

Grace slowed her steps as she followed Alex into the room and let her gaze drift over the large, framed photographs of breathtaking scenes hanging on the walls. The huge pictures offered a panoramic view of some of the most famous places in the world, places she'd always wanted to visit. Leather couches and chairs with tables beside them were scattered across the area where several people who Grace assumed to be clients sat reading newspapers or magazines.

A huge Christmas tree, its white lights twinkling like tiny diamonds and ornaments dangling from every branch, took up a whole corner of the massive room. The halo of the angel at the top touched the ceiling, and packages wrapped in gold paper sat underneath. A cart next to the tree was loaded with coffee carafes, Christmas cookies, pastries and fruit.

The receptionist smiled at them as she and Alex approached her desk. "May I help you?"

Alex pulled out his badge and showed it to the young woman. "I'm Detective Crowne with the Memphis Police. This is Grace Kincaid from WKIZ. I called earlier this morning. Mr. Jefferson is expecting us."

The woman's smile grew larger. "Mr. Jefferson told me you were coming. He's with a client right now, but I'll let you know when he's available. In the meantime, help yourself to the food on the cart."

Alex nodded and headed to the coffee cart, but Grace stepped closer to the receptionist's desk. "I couldn't help but notice all these beautiful framed photographs on the wall. I'd love to have some for my home. Would you mind telling me where you bought them?"

The woman laughed and shook her head. "I'm afraid you can't buy them anywhere. They're all Mr. Jefferson's work."

"Really? Sam shot all those pictures?"

"Yes. He's quite the photographer, and he

loves to travel. He took them all while he was on trips."

"I'll have to tell him how beautiful they are," Grace murmured. She glanced around at Alex who balanced a cup of coffee in one hand and a Christmas cookie with thick icing in the other as he eased onto a sofa.

He glanced up as she sat down beside him. "This cookie is good. Want one?"

She shook her head. "No, thanks."

"They have eggnog, too."

"I'll wait. It's almost lunchtime."

"I know, but I didn't have time for breakfast this morning. I need something to tide me over until we go to lunch."

His words left a question in her mind. Did he mean they would eat together or go their separate ways after seeing Sam? She directed her eyes to her hands clenched in her lap. "You've done so much for me over the past few days, I'd like to take you to lunch."

He washed a bite of cookie down with a swig of coffee and nodded. "Okay. Where would you like to go?"

She thought for a moment before she answered. "A new tea room just opened down on Madison. Laura and I had lunch there the other day, and the food was delicious. They have all kinds of salads and sandwiches."

He swallowed another sip of coffee. "Do they have barbecue?"

She frowned. "Barbecue? I don't think so."

"So they don't have *all kinds* of sandwiches. Just chick food that's on some kind of bread I can't pronounce and a veggie substitute inside instead of meat."

Her face grew warm, and she leaned closer. "Well, pardon me. I forgot you live and breathe barbecue. Tell me where you want to go, and I'll take you there."

He laughed, and several people in the waiting area turned to look at them. "I'm sorry, Grace. I couldn't resist teasing you a bit. You always wanted to introduce me to the culinary delights of Memphis as you called them, but I'm still a meat and potatoes kind of guy. And there's nothing better to me than Memphis barbecue."

She burst out laughing at the twinkle in his eye. "I know, Alex, and I won't try to change you. Since I'm treating you, we'll go wherever you want. Where will it be?"

He studied her for a moment, then a slow smile spread across his face. "I think I'd like to try the tea room on Madison. Maybe it's time for some changes in my life."

His gaze caressed her face as it traveled from her eyes to her lips, where it lingered for a moment before he took a quick breath and settled back on the sofa. Grace eased back into the cushions, picked up a magazine from the table next to the couch and held it in front of her face. What had just happened between her and Alex? Just now they'd laughed and joked together as they had years ago. Was it possible they could become friends again?

Before she could dwell any longer on the relationship changes she and Alex appeared to be experiencing, the receptionist rose from her desk and motioned for them. "Mr. Jefferson will see you now."

Alex drained the last drop of coffee from his cup and rose to follow Grace. When they reached the desk, the young woman took the cup and set it on a tray beside the door before she led them down a long hallway. They stopped in front of a mahogany door, and she knocked.

"Come in." The muffled voice came from inside.

She opened the door, stepped aside and motioned for them to enter. Grace eased into the room with Alex right behind her. Sam Jefferson rose from the chair behind his desk and held out his hand. "Alex, Grace. It's good to see you again." He shook both their hands and motioned them to the chairs in front of his desk, then he sat down.

Alex propped his elbows on the arms of his chair and leaned forward. "Thanks for seeing us on such short notice, Sam. From the looks of people waiting, it must be a busy day around here."

Sam shook his head. "No more than usual. But I always have time for old friends. I don't think I've seen you since we graduated." He glanced at Grace. "Of course I see you on the news every day, but that's not the same. How have you been doing?"

Grace smiled. "I'm fine."

He leaned back in his chair. "And how's your father doing? I heard about the drive-by shooting. I hope he's recovered and doing all right."

"He lived, but he'll spend the rest of his life in a wheelchair. That's been difficult for him to accept, but I think he has now."

Sam's eyes grew wide. "I had no idea." He stared at her for a moment before he cleared his throat and turned to Alex. "And I read in the paper you're heading up a new unit at the police department with Brad Austin and another detective."

Alex nodded. "A Cold Case Unit. Seth Dawtry

is the other officer who works with Brad and me. In fact, Grace and I are here today about a case the police have never closed."

"Oh? Which one?"

"Landon Mitchell's death."

Sam's face paled, and he clasped his hands on top of his desk. "I thought Landon's death was ruled a suicide."

Alex shook his head. "Suicide was suspected but never proved. If you saw Grace's coverage earlier this week, you know Landon's father jumped from the Memphis-Arkansas Bridge. Before he did, he made some accusations we're looking into."

Sam shifted in his chair and narrowed his eyes. "What kind of accusations?"

"He said he suspected Landon was involved with a secret group of some kind before his death. Mr. Mitchell found lots of money hidden in his son's room, and he also saw a wolf tattooed on his shoulder." Alex paused and took a breath. "We thought you might know something about these things."

Sam regarded Alex with an aloof expression and shrugged. "Why would I know anything? I barely knew Landon."

Grace sat up straight and gasped. "Sam, how

can you say that? Our senior year you were with him all the time."

Sam directed a frosty glare in her direction, and a shiver went up Grace's spine. "I had a lot of friends. Landon was one of them, but we didn't hang out together after school. In fact, I found him rather boring."

"So these other friends you had," Alex interrupted. "Would they have been Jeremy Baker, Billy Warren, Clay Mercer and Dustin Shelton?"

Sam picked up a pencil from the desk and began to roll it in his fingers. "Yes, they were friends of mine."

"Did you know that Jeremy, Billy and Dustin are all dead, too?"

"Yes. I was sad when I heard about each of them."

Alex leaned forward. "Don't you think it's strange that four boys you were friends with in school have all died."

Sam shook his head. "Not necessarily. Everybody dies, Alex. Some sooner than others."

"Do you know if any of them had a wolf tattooed on their shoulders?" Alex's stare didn't waver from Sam's face.

Sam didn't flinch but returned an icy glare. "I have no idea."

Alex let his gaze drop to Sam's shoulder.

"What about you? Do you have a wolf tattooed on yours?"

Sam rose to his feet, tossed the pencil he held to the desk, and glanced at his watch. "I'm afraid I'm going to have to cut our visit short. I have paying clients waiting to see me."

Alex and Grace rose as Sam walked over to the door and opened it. "It was good seeing you two again. Maybe we'll meet at the next reunion of our graduating class."

Alex trailed Grace to the door and stopped in front of Sam. "I'm going to find out what happened to Landon, Sam. If you think of anything that might help, give me a call at the station."

"I will."

"Goodbye, Sam," Grace said as she and Alex walked from the office.

They had only taken a few steps when Sam's voice called out. "Oh, Alex."

They stopped and turned to face him. "Yes?" Alex said.

"For your information I've always been afraid of needles. I have no tattoo."

Before they could answer, he closed the door. They looked at the door then back to each other and walked from the office. They didn't speak until they'd climbed into Alex's car. Then Grace swiveled in her seat and faced him. "What did you make of our visit?"

Alex smiled and shook his head. "He knows something. He tried to hide it under his courtroom facade, but my question about the tattoo rattled him."

"What will we do now?"

"Let's give him a few days to stew over what we told him. Then we'll come back. In the meantime, how would you like to take a trip to Nashville to see Clay?"

"That sounds like a great idea. When do you want to go?"

"I don't know. With the holidays Clay may be back in Memphis. I'll check tomorrow and let you know." He turned the key in the ignition. "Now how about some lunch? I'm starved."

Grace laughed and nodded. "You're the chauffeur. Go wherever you like."

He grinned, and Grace's heart fluttered at the boyish teasing that sparkled in his eyes. From somewhere deep inside her a memory surfaced. She remembered how she used to run the tip of her index finger down his jawline, and how he would smile in contentment when she did. She couldn't move for a moment, and then she blinked and took a deep breath. She couldn't let herself think like that. Right now she needed to concentrate on finding the man whose attempts on her life had turned it into a living nightmare. Then she could go back to her peaceful life, and Alex could go to Florida.

Alex leaned back into the plush sofa cushions in the Kincaids' den and stretched his legs out in front of him. Dinner at the Kincaid house had been delicious as he'd known it would be, and conversation with Harrison had proved interesting. He couldn't believe he was actually beginning to like the man. Now as he waited for Grace to return from helping her mother put her father to bed he was glad for a few minutes alone to reflect on what was happening in his life.

A week ago he'd been content to go to work every day and search old files in the hopes some piece of overlooked information would leap off the page and send him in pursuit of someone who'd gotten away with murder years before. Then he'd been called to the bridge where a man was threatening suicide, and Grace had reentered his life.

Now he was beginning to feel comfortable around her again, and he couldn't let that happen. He didn't believe for one minute that she'd stay in Memphis if her father's condition improved. She'd be knocking at the networks' doors again to get her old job back, and he really couldn't blame her. She was the total package when it came to what the networks wanted in an anchor. She was beautiful, smart and had the ability to connect with viewers.

He jumped to his feet, strode to the window and looked outside. The question remained, what was he going to do? Did he really want to give up his job in Memphis to go to Florida? He really missed his father and would like to be with him again. He sighed and leaned against the window frame. It wouldn't hurt to apply for the job down there. There was no guarantee he'd get it. Perhaps he should apply and see what happened.

"What are you doing?" Grace's voice startled him, and he glanced over his shoulder to see her entering the room.

"Just looking outside. Did you get your father settled?"

She nodded. "He said to say good-night for him and tell you he was glad you came to dinner again. He's enjoying getting to know you."

"It's good to see this side of him, too." A glow lit her face, and he let his gaze drift over her. She'd never looked more beautiful. He swallowed and turned back to look outside. "The weatherman says we may get some more snow next week."

She eased up beside him and looked out into the night. "I hope so. Do you remember how we used to wish for snow at Christmas when we were children?"

They stood so close he could smell her perfume, which gave off a fruity fragrance. "I remember, but we're not children anymore, Grace."

A sad look flickered in her eyes. "No, we're not. I suppose going back to the school yesterday brought up a lot of old memories and a lot of unexplained reasons for why things turned out the way they did between us."

His heart pounded, and he shook his head. "Grace, please, I don't want to talk about this."

"There's something I want to ask you. Did you ever wish you had gotten in touch with me after we broke up?"

He nodded. "I did. But then I could ask you the same question. Did you wish you had called me?"

"Yes." The word was barely a whisper.

His eyebrows arched at her answer. What had made him wait so long? Pride? Anger? He had no answer, but it really didn't matter. There was no going back and making everything right again.

He sighed. "Well, neither of us did, and we both survived. I have a great job here in Memphis, and you went on to New York and built a great career in television as an investigative reporter and then a news anchor. I imagine when your father improves you'll be off to the networks to continue your career, and I'll be happy for you."

Her eyes filled with tears. "I don't know if—"

The ringing of his cell phone interrupted what she was about to say, and he pulled the phone from his pocket. He glanced at the caller ID and frowned. "It's our office phone." He connected the call. "Hello."

"Alex, it's Seth."

"Hey, man. Are you still at the office?"

"Yeah, I've been looking over the files from the Mitchell case."

"Did you find anything?"

"No, I called to tell you something else. I know when you called in this morning you said you and Grace were going downtown to some lawyer's office."

"Yes. Sam Jefferson's."

"I thought Jefferson was the guy's name."

Alex frowned and glanced at Grace. "What makes you ask about Sam?"

"One of the homicide detectives I used to

work with dropped by the office a few minutes ago and told me they found Sam Jefferson's body earlier tonight in the parking lot at his office building. He said it looked like he'd been shot execution-style in the back of the head when he was getting in his car."

The breath exploded from Alex's body in a rush, and he clamped his hand over his eyes. "No, no. This can't be true."

"I'm afraid it is, buddy. Sorry I have to tell you."

Alex took a deep breath. "Don't worry about it." He pulled the phone away from his ear and looked at Grace. "The police found Sam Jefferson shot to death." Her mouth dropped open, and she sank onto the couch. Alex turned his attention back to Seth. "Are the police still at the scene?"

"I think the crime scene investigators are there now. The medical examiner has the body."

"Thanks for calling, Seth. I'll see you in the morning."

He ended the call and sat down beside Grace on the couch. "What happened?" she asked.

Alex related what Seth had told him and took a deep breath. "I need to make another call." He punched in the number he'd called so many times in his years on the force. Dr. Harvey answered on the first ring.

"Medical examiner's office. Dr. Harvey speaking."

"Dr. Harvey, this is Alex Crowne. I understand you've brought Sam Jefferson's body to your office."

"Yes, Alex, but I haven't done any work yet."

"I realize that, but there's something I'd like for you to check for me first. It may shed some light on a cold case I'm working."

"What is it?"

"Would you check the victim's shoulders and see if he has a wolf tattooed on either one?"

"Sure, Alex. Give me a minute."

Alex drummed his fingers on the sofa cushion as he waited for Dr. Harvey to return. Within minutes his voice came over the phone. "Alex?"

"Yes?"

"I checked, and he does indeed have a wolf tattoo. Do you want me to take some pictures of it and email them to you?"

"I would appreciate it very much. Thanks, Doc."

"No problem."

Alex disconnected the call and nodded. "He has the same tattoo Landon had. I think Mr. Mitchell must have been right. Those boys became involved in some kind of secret society and used the wolf as its symbol. And now five of the six are dead. We need to get to Clay as soon as possible. He may be next on the killer's list."

"I think you're right," Grace said.

"Or..." Alex paused. "As the only survivor, he may be the killer who's trying to protect some secret."

Grace only nodded, but he could tell his words concerned her. She hadn't forgotten, and neither had he, that someone out there had also tried to kill her. It had to be tied into whatever Landon Mitchell and his friends had done twelve years ago. He hoped he could find the answer before someone else was silenced.

NINE

In the early afternoon the next day, Alex and Grace sped along Interstate 40 on the three-hour drive from Memphis to Nashville. Neither had spoken for the past fifteen minutes, and Grace didn't think she could endure the silence much longer. She glanced at Alex out of the corner of her eye and saw the muscle in his jaw twitch, a sign he was in deep thought. What was going on in his head? Was he upset over Sam's death, or was it something else? Their interrupted conversation last night might be the reason for his silence.

She took a deep breath and swiveled in her seat to face him. "I'm surprised you were able to reach Clay. I thought surely he would already have left Nashville for the holidays."

Alex nodded. "I thought so, too. He said he and his wife are leaving later today for a skiing trip. They're spending the holidays in Germany."

"Probably in Garmisch. Our families used to

see each other there on skiing vacations. His father and mine loved skiing the trails of the Zugspitzplatt. It's a beautiful place."

"I wouldn't know. I've never taken a ski trip. For that matter, I never learned to ski."

"It's not too late, you know. You can still learn."

He chuckled and shook his head. "Not on a policeman's salary. Can't afford it."

"Sure you can. There are a lot of places around that don't cost all that much. You could go there while you're saving up for a bigger trip later on."

He cast a sideways glance at her before he turned his attention back to the highway. "I don't think so. Besides, there aren't many ski resorts in Florida."

His words hit her like a punch in the stomach. She took a deep breath. "So you're really going to move."

He nodded. "I'm considering it. It makes sense. Even if I don't get the chief of police job, I'm sure I can get on with one of the law enforcement agencies down there, and I can take care of my father."

"I see. If that's what you want, I wish you well."

She closed her eyes and settled back in her seat. The sound of the tires on the pavement lulled her, and she began to nod. The next thing she knew, Alex was shaking her shoulder. "Wake up, Grace. We're at the restaurant where I told Clay we would meet him."

She sat up and rubbed her eyes. The afternoon sun had begun to sink into the west, and shadows stretched across the parking lot. Christmas lights around the roofline of the restaurant twinkled in the coming darkness.

She unbuckled her seat belt, pulled the sun visor down and looked in the mirror on the back. "The days are so short in winter. By five o'clock it'll be dark, and then we have the drive home."

"I may let you drive back to Memphis so I can sleep like you did on the way to Nashville."

She glanced around at him, and her heart thumped at his grin. "As long as you feed me, I can do that."

He surveyed the restaurant. "Clay mentioned dinner, but I don't know when he has to leave for the airport. If he can't stay, we'll eat anyway."

"I just hope he understands the urgency of what we have to ask him. We don't want him to end up like all his friends."

Alex held up a finger as if to caution her. "Unless he's the killer. Remember that, and watch his every move. Also remember I have no jurisdiction here. This is strictly a meeting to question him about what he knows. He's not required to answer anything I ask him."

She swallowed her fear. "Do you really think he could have been the one who tried to kill me?"

"I don't know. At this point I'd say with his connection to the other victims, we could consider him a person of interest."

Grace nodded and opened the car door. Together they walked to the front door and entered the restaurant. Soft Christmas music drifted through the interior, and a decorated tree graced one corner of the entry. A young woman dressed in a knee-length full black skirt and a white blouse with billowing sleeves buttoned at the wrists greeted them.

"Good evening. Welcome to Antonio's. Do you have a reservation?"

Alex nodded. "Yes. It's in Clay Mercer's name."

Her eyes lit in recognition, and she smiled. "Mr. Mercer's been here for a while. I'll show you to his table."

As they followed the hostess to the table, Grace let her gaze drift over the restaurant. Since it would be several hours before the dinner crowd arrived, there were only a few customers seated at the elegantly draped tables adorned with flickering candles. Waiters and waitresses in their black pants with matching vests and white shirts bustled about the room as they prepared for expected customers.

Grace caught sight of Clay halfway across the room, and he waved to them. The boy whose family had shared vacations with the Kincaids was hardly visible in the man with the receding hairline and expanding waistline. He staggered a bit as he rose and clasped her hand when she stopped beside the table.

"Grace Kincaid. I can't believe it's you. I haven't seen you in years." Clay's slurred words rolled from his mouth. The smell of alcohol on his breath let Grace know how Clay had spent his time waiting for them.

"It has been a long time, Clay." She shook his hand and then eased into the chair Alex held for her next to Clay. She cast a smile over her shoulder. "Thanks, Alex."

Clay's gaze drifted back to Alex, and he reached out and shook his hand. "And Alex. Good to see you, too. I don't think I've seen you since graduation."

"It has been a while."

Clay motioned for Alex to have a seat, then picked up his glass and swallowed what was left of his drink. With a cocky smile he held up the empty glass. "Marjorie, darling, find out what my friends are drinking and bring me one of these."

Concern flickered in Marjorie's eyes, and she hesitated. "Mr. Mercer, you're already over your limit. Maybe you need to order something to eat."

His eyes narrowed, and his face flushed. "Don't tell me what I need. Just do what I say."

Marjorie's lips trembled, and she cast a quick look at Grace. "But Antonio said—"

Clay slammed the glass down on the table and glared at her. "I don't care what he said. I'm the customer, and I told you what I wanted."

Grace smiled reassuringly at Marjorie. "All I want to drink is a glass of water." She glanced up at Clay. "And I am a bit hungry. I'd really like to order. What about you, Alex?"

"Water's fine for me, too." He smiled at the hostess. "If you'll have the waiter come over, we'll order."

Marjorie cast a grateful smile in their direction and hurried away from the table. Clay shook his head and frowned as he sank back into his chair. "I keep telling Antonio he should get better help in here, but he won't listen to me."

Grace started to respond, but the waiter arrived at that moment to tell them the specials of the day. After ordering, Clay slumped back in his seat and looked from Grace to Alex. "Okay, so let's have it. I don't think a TV anchor and a police detective drove all the way from Memphis to Nashville just to have a reunion with a high school classmate. What do you two really want?"

Alex leaned forward and crossed his arms on top of the table. "We want to talk to you about Landon Mitchell."

Clay picked up his water glass and took a drink. When he set it back on the table, it wobbled, and he grabbed it to keep it from turning over. "Are you talking about the kid who committed suicide when we were in high school?"

"Yes."

Clay shrugged. "I don't know how I can help. I barely knew him."

Grace shook her head. "That's not true, Clay. You and Landon were inseparable our senior year. I saw the two of you together all the time."

"We were lab partners in chemistry class. We were only together to study." He reached for his glass again, and his hand shook.

Grace reached over and placed her hand on his arm. "Clay, Landon didn't take chemistry our senior year."

His face grew red, and he glared at her. "Yes, he did."

"No, he didn't. I know what his schedule was because it was just like mine. And he didn't take chemistry."

He shook free of her and shrugged. "Then maybe I'm mixed up. It must have been our junior year. Anyway, what does a twelve-year-old suicide have to do with me?"

Alex's stare bored into Clay. "It's strange, isn't it, that so many of the kids we graduated with are dead now."

"Wh-what do you mean?" Clay asked.

Alex pursed his lips as if in deep thought. "Well, there's Landon, of course, and Jeremy, Billy and Dustin. You remember all of them, don't you?"

Clay picked up his drink glass and frowned at the empty container. "Of course I remember them."

"And now Sam Jefferson."

Clay's mouth twitched, and he swallowed before he set the glass back on the table. "Sam's dead?"

Alex nodded. "Yes. He was murdered yesterday."

Grace had expected a violent reaction from Clay, but it didn't happen. Instead, he sat perfectly still. After a moment, he took a deep breath. "What do you really want from me, Alex?"

Alex leaned forward. "For starters, Clay, I'd like to know if you have a wolf tattooed on your shoulder."

He shook his head. "No, I don't."

"Landon did, and so did Sam."

Clay sighed. "I wouldn't know anything about that."

Alex didn't blink as he stared at Clay. "Would you be willing to prove it to me?"

Clay frowned and shook his head. "Why should I have to prove anything to you?"

"Because then we'll know you weren't part of the group that had the tattoos."

Clay pushed his chair back from the table and glanced at them. "You don't have any proof that I know anything about Landon's death or you'd have a warrant. Now why don't we agree to have dinner as three old friends and leave it at that?"

Alex shook his head. "Because right now the Memphis police are investigating Sam's murder. You're going to have to talk to them at some point. Why not do it now instead of later?"

Clay worried his lip and looked at Grace. "I'm really sorry about Sam. He was a good friend.

It looks like I'm the only one of our group of friends left."

Grace nodded. "If you know anything that can help Alex find out who killed Sam, you need to tell him."

He shook his head. "I don't know anything about Sam's murder or what happened to the others." He glanced down at his glass again and sighed. "All this talk has made me thirsty. I sure could use another drink before dinner. I don't care what Marjorie and Antonio say." He rose and laid his napkin on the table. "I'm going to speak with the bartender. I'll be back in a minute."

Grace's gaze followed him as he strode across the dining room. When he disappeared into the bar area, she looked at Alex and frowned. "He seemed genuinely sorry about Sam's death. Do you think he could be the murderer?"

Alex shrugged. "I don't know. Maybe he'll say something else while we're eating that will shed some light on this case. I just hope the bartender doesn't give him another drink. His blood alcohol is probably already too high to drive."

Grace nodded and glanced around the room. Several tables had filled while they'd been talking with Clay. Her wandering gaze locked on a young couple a few tables away from them. A large Christmas shopping bag sat in the empty chair next to the woman, and she smiled as she pulled out a doll and passed it to the man. His eyes lit up, and he nodded and smiled as he examined the toy. Her heart lurched. They must be a married couple, and the woman had just purchased the doll for their daughter's Christmas present. How happy they looked.

She shifted her gaze to Alex and struggled to keep tears from filling her eyes. If things had worked out for them, she and Alex might very well be discussing Christmas presents for their children. Instead, all that drew them together this Christmas were some unsolved murders and attempts on her life.

"Excuse me." A voice interrupted her thoughts, and she glanced up to see Marjorie standing by their table. "Mr. Mercer asked me to give you a message."

Alex's gaze darted past her to the entrance to the bar. "Is there a problem?"

She nodded. "I'm afraid so. He asked me to tell you he received an urgent phone call and had to leave. Your dinner is paid for, and it will be here in a few minutes. He said for you to enjoy your time here and he'll phone you when he gets back from Germany."

Alex let out a long breath. "Thank you for telling us."

Grace waited for Marjorie to leave before she spoke. "Can you believe that?"

"I should have suspected he was up to something and gone with him." The look on his face reminded Grace of how Alex used to look when she beat him at one of the board games they loved. Amusement bubbled up in her. She pressed her hand against her mouth, but it was no use. A loud burst of laughter escaped her lips. He frowned. "What's the matter?"

She struggled to quiet down. "I was just thinking we are pathetic. Here you are a police detective who deals with criminals all the time and I'm a journalist who interviews people from all walks of life. We're trained to tell when people are lying, and neither one of us tried to stop Clay from walking out of here."

He regarded her with a serious look for a moment, then his lips pulled into a grin. A sheepish expression covered his face. "You're right. We let him outsmart us. We'll have to be more careful in the future."

Her laughter died, and she crossed her arms on top of the table. "Do you think we'll get the chance to question him again?"

Alex nodded. "Oh, yeah. And the next time he won't get away so easily."

Two waiters appeared at their table just as he finished speaking. The smells from the covered plates they carried made Grace's stomach growl, and she pressed her hand to her abdomen. "Mmm, that smells good."

The waiters set the plates in front of them and removed their covers. "Is everything satisfactory?" one of them asked.

"Mine looks scrumptious," Grace said.

"And my steak is perfect," Alex added.

When the two men had left, Grace picked up her fork and knife and cut off a bite of chicken. Before she could raise it to her mouth, Alex spoke. "Grace?"

She halted, her fork in midair, and looked up at him. His gaze drifted over her face, and her skin tingled. "Yes?"

"I've enjoyed being with you these past few days."

She swallowed and nodded. "I've enjoyed it, too."

"I'm kind of glad Clay ran out on us. He's not here, and we're not at the table with your parents. Tonight we can just enjoy being together."

Before she could respond, he looked back at his plate and began to cut into his steak. She smiled and dropped her gaze back to her plate. Over the past few days she and Alex had become more comfortable around each other, and she was glad. Their friendship had been the best part of her childhood, and she hoped they could eventually reach the place where they could lay the bad memories of their adulthood to rest.

With a sigh she raised her fork to her lips and closed them around the bite of chicken.

Alex relaxed behind the wheel of the car and hummed along with the music of his favorite Memphis radio station as he cruised along Interstate 40. He glanced over at Grace sleeping soundly in the passenger seat and smiled.

It seemed so right to have her in the car with him. He'd been lonely since their breakup, and a day didn't go by without some memory of her popping into his head. Some days it might have been an angry thought, but most of the time it was about the good times they'd spent together, especially during their childhood.

She groaned in her sleep, and he jerked his head to glance at her. A look as if she were in pain flashed across her face, and she moaned again. "No, no."

He reached over and gave her a gentle shake. "Grace, are you all right?"

Her eyes blinked open. She looked at him with a wild-eyed stare and sat up straight in her seat. "Alex…"

"I'm here, Grace."

She turned her head from side to side as if to get her bearings and rubbed her hands over her eyes. She exhaled a deep breath. "Where are we?"

"Just outside of Memphis. You called out in your sleep."

She yawned and settled back in her seat. "I must have been dreaming. I don't know what it was, though."

"We should be at your house before too long. You can go right to bed."

She shook her head. "No, I'll have to wait up for my parents. They went to see the church's Christmas program tonight. In fact, they took our maid and cook with them, as well. There shouldn't be anybody at home when I get there."

"Then maybe I'd better stay until they get home."

She glanced at the clock on the car dashboard. "If you don't mind, I'd appreciate your doing that. I didn't think I'd ever be afraid to stay alone. I suppose those two attempts to kill me have changed my mind, but my parents should be home soon. I'm sorry to be such a nuisance."

He nodded and kept his attention directed to the traffic, which had increased since they got closer to the city. "You aren't a nuisance. You've been a lot braver than most people would have been in your situation. I'm glad to see that you're finally beginning to be cautious instead of charging in without thinking."

"Oh, is that what you think I do? Charge in without thinking?"

He chuckled. "I'd say that's right. Do you remember the time when we were about twelve years old and you decided you wanted a soft drink and there weren't any in the refrigerator in the kitchen?"

She laughed. "So I decided to borrow my mother's car and drive down to the convenience store and get some for you and me to drink."

"Yeah. I tried to talk you out of it, but you wouldn't listen."

"And you were afraid for me go alone," Grace continued, "so you jumped in the car with me so you could help me if anything happened."

By this time they were both laughing. Alex glanced at her. "And we didn't make it down the driveway before you hit a tree."

Grace lay back in the seat and shook her head. "I don't think I've ever seen my father so angry. I was grounded for weeks."

"As well you deserved to be." They rode in silence for a few minutes, each lost in their own thoughts, before Alex spoke again. "We have some great memories, Grace."

"Yes, we do," she whispered and turned to gaze out the window.

Thirty minutes later he pulled the car to a stop at the gate to Grace's house and typed in the code. The big iron gates opened, and he drove through the entrance to the walled Kincaid estate. He watched in the rearview mirror as the gates closed automatically behind him.

Beside him, Grace leaned forward in her seat and looked through the windshield. "That's strange."

"What is?"

She pointed toward the house. "Look. Every light in the house is on."

He stared straight ahead and frowned at the bright beams shining through every window. The house practically glowed it was so lit up. "Is that unusual?"

She nodded. "My parents are always after me to turn out a light when I leave a room to conserve energy. There's no way they would have left home with every bulb in the house burning."

"Are you sure? Maybe they wanted the outside Christmas decorations to show up."

She shook her head. "I know my parents. They would never have left all those lights on."

Alex pulled the car to a stop at the front of the house and got out. Grace jumped out and fumbled in her purse for her key as she ran toward the front steps. He raced around the front of the vehicle and caught her arm just as she started up the steps. "Wait, Grace. Let me go first."

She turned back to him, her eyes wide. "Why? Do you think something's wrong?"

He stepped in front of her and pulled his gun from the holster. "I don't know, but I need to check this out before we go bursting in there."

She gasped, and her hand covered her mouth. "Do you think someone could be in there?"

"Could be. Go ahead and unlock the door for me, but wait on the porch. I'll be back in a few minutes."

She nodded and started to stick the key in the door but turned back to him. "The door's open. It looks like somebody jimmied it."

He pulled her away from the door, reached for his cell phone and dialed 911. When the operator answered, he identified himself. "I need backup for a B and E at 3947 Tulip Grove Road. I'm entering the house now." He glanced over his shoulder at Grace. "Drive my car back to the gate and open it for the police. Don't come inside the house until we've cleared it."

She nodded and backed away. He waited until she drove down the driveway before he entered the house. Holding the gun in front of him, he eased inside and swept it back and forth as he surveyed the scene before him. The home looked as if a whirlwind had ripped through it. Sofas and chairs, their pillows cut open and the stuffing pulled out, lay overturned amid upended tables and shattered lamps. Picture frames with their glass broken out hung at crooked angles on the wall.

In the den the Christmas tree lay on its side, its broken ornaments scattered across the floor. The Christmas presents had been opened, and the items that had been inside littered the floor.

The sound of a police siren split the air, and he pulled out his badge. He'd just arrived at the front door when the first patrol car pulled to a stop. He held his badge up as the officers jumped out of the cruiser. "I'm Detective Alex Crowne. I've cleared the front rooms downstairs, but I haven't been upstairs or checked the back of the house."

Two more cars with Grace trailing behind rolled to a stop, and officers rushed to the porch.

The officer in charge nodded to Alex. "Thanks. We'll take it from here."

Alex moved out of the way and met Grace at the bottom of the steps. "Was there anyone inside?"

"I didn't see anyone, but the officers are checking." He took a deep breath. "Grace, it looks bad in there. It looks like somebody took their time and moved from room to room trashing everything in their path."

Her eyes filled with tears, and she started toward the porch. He grabbed her arm and pulled her back. "You can't go in there yet. The police are still working, and you need to be prepared when you see it."

She turned back to him, and his heart thudded at the fear in her eyes. "It's the killer, isn't it? I've survived his attempts to kill me, so he wants to hurt me in another way by destroying my home. Why does he hate me so?"

"I don't know." A wail escaped her throat, and she covered her eyes with her hands as the tears rolled down her cheeks. Her shoulders shook, and before he realized what he was doing, he had wrapped his arms around her and pulled her close. She laid her head against his chest, and he tightened his arms. "Don't cry. It's going to be all right."

She pulled back and stared up into his eyes. "It's not going to be all right. I should have listened to you. You warned me about getting involved in Landon's death, and now I've brought more misery on my parents. They have enough to face with my father's condition. In the past week they've had to worry about me almost being killed twice, and now they're going to come back to a vandalized home. They don't deserve this."

She sagged against him, and her head dropped to his chest. He didn't know what to say that would comfort her. This latest development probably was related to the Mitchell case, but it also told him something else. Mr. Mitchell had been right about his son being murdered, and he and Grace must have gotten close to some answers. But if Landon's killer had come into the Kincaids' house, he had to know they wouldn't be home and he had to know how to access the property some way other than through the main gate.

Perhaps the killer knew more about the Kincaids than Alex had thought. He could have been watching them all along. He tightened his arms around Grace and looked out into the dark night. "Don't worry, Grace," he whispered. "I promise you we'll get this guy."

TEN

An hour after coming home to the chaos inside the house, Grace stood on the front porch, two suitcases at her feet, and scanned the driveway leading from the now-open gate. Police cars, some with their blue lights still flashing, were parked up and down the driveway. From time to time she could hear voices inside the house and wondered if the officers had found any clues as to who had invaded their home.

The front door opened, and Alex stepped onto the porch. "I thought I'd check and see if your parents had gotten here yet."

She shook her head. "Mom called when they left the church to see if I'd gotten home, and I told her what had happened. They're on their way now."

He glanced down at the suitcases. "Were you able to find enough clothes for all of you to take with you?"

"Yes. There had been some left in the closets of the bedrooms, and I collected enough for overnight. I called the Peabody and reserved us a suite with two bedrooms, and I called the drugstore." Anger flowed through her, and she clenched her hands at her sides. "Why did he have to pour all my father's medications in the toilet and then not flush it? It was almost like a taunt to see his medicine in the water and know it was useless to help with pain if needed."

"I know. I've seen burglars and vandals do a lot of crazy things. It's hard to know the mindset of someone like that. What did the pharmacist say when you talked with him?"

Grace let out a long breath. "I explained the situation, and he said we could get enough medicine to get us through the night. We'll contact the doctor in the morning for new prescriptions."

"Good." Alex stared toward the gate as a vehicle turned into the driveway. "Is that your folks' van?"

"No, that's the WKIZ van."

He turned to her and frowned. "What's it doing here?"

"I called Derek, the cameraman that came to the bridge with me, and asked him to come over and bring a reporter."

"Why?"

Grace steeled herself for Alex's anger when

she told him what she had planned. "I'm going to do a live feed on the ten o'clock news."

"You're what?" The words exploded out of Alex's mouth.

"I talked with the producer, and he okayed it. I'm going to let the person who did this know he can't scare me. We may not be able to prove it yet, but I know whoever did this killed Landon and a lot of other people."

Alex raked his hand through his hair. "Grace, I don't think—"

She reached out and grasped his arm. "Alex, this guy has killed people we went to school with, he's attempted to kill me and now he's violated the security of my home. Reporting is my job, and I have to cover this story."

After a moment he nodded, then directed his gaze back down the driveway where a second vehicle had just entered. "Tell that to your folks. Here they come." He picked up the suitcases and waited for her parents' van to come to a stop.

Grace walked down the steps with Alex behind her, motioned for Derek to park beside the house, and waited for her mother to stop next to her. She then opened the sliding door on the side and peered in at her father strapped in his wheelchair.

She reached in and grasped his outstretched

hand. "The police haven't finished inside yet, so there's no need for you to come in. Go on to the Peabody, but don't forget the medicine at the drugstore. The pharmacist said he'd have it at the drive-through. I'll meet you at the hotel when I can leave here."

Her father shook his head. "I don't want you driving downtown alone."

Alex shoved the two bags into the van and glanced at Grace. "Don't worry, sir. I'll drive Grace down there and see that she's settled."

Grace frowned. "Alex, that's not—"

He held up his hand to stop her. "I insist. No discussion needed."

Her parents exchanged quick glances, and a smile pulled at her father's lips. "Thanks, Alex. It seems like I'm thanking you a lot lately for taking care of my daughter." His gaze drifted to the house. "For years I worked day and night to buy the things I thought would make my family happy. Now I realize those were just possessions. There's nothing in that house that can even start to compare with the safety of my wife and daughter. I wish I had learned that lesson sooner."

Grace patted his hand and smiled. "Don't think about that now, Dad. You go with Mother, and I'll see the two of you later."

She and Alex watched as her mother turned the van around and drove back toward the gate. When the van turned onto the road leading toward the city, Alex looked at her and shook his head. "I still can't believe how much your father has changed. He's not the same man I knew."

"I know. That's what happens when God takes over in someone's life. He becomes a new person."

"I've heard that, but I never thought it possible. Now I've seen it with my own eyes. It makes me wish I could be more like your father."

She smiled up at him. "You can, Alex. All you have to do is open up your heart to God."

He shrugged. "I'll think about it." He glanced past her and frowned. "Here comes the cameraman. It's not too late to change your mind."

She turned to smile at Derek, but her mouth opened in surprise at the sight of Julie Colter walking with him. They came to a stop beside her, and she glanced from one to the other. "Julie, what a surprise. I didn't expect to see you."

Julie bit down on her lip and glanced up at Derek. "Well, you see..." She hesitated and turned to Derek.

Derek shifted the camera he was carrying in

his arms and smiled at Julie "She's going to do your interview."

Grace's eyes grew wide. "Wh-what?"

Derek nodded. "Julie's been talking to me at the station, and she's not cut out for what management has her doing. They told her she'd get a chance to prove herself with some public interest stories. So far they haven't followed through on their promise. How about it, Grace? Let's give her a chance."

Grace blinked and searched her mind for something to say. Did she really want klutzy Julie to do this interview? Since the girl had arrived at the station, she'd made so many mistakes the station manager was about to fire her.

Before she could reply to Derek's question, Julie lifted her chin and took a deep breath. "I know I've made some mistakes, Miss Kincaid, but nobody has ever really given me any guidance. I've tried to do what I thought the manager wanted, but I haven't seemed to please him. I have a degree in journalism, and I worked at my college's TV station as a reporter. In fact, I won some awards, but he won't give me an assignment. Derek is trying to help me out. I'd be forever grateful if you would, too."

Grace cast a helpless glance at Alex who shrugged and then to Derek before she locked gazes with Julie. "But this is a live feed into the news which is in progress right now. There'll be no do-overs, and we can't correct any mistakes we make. Do you understand?"

Julie nodded, and the plea that sparkled in her eyes reminded Grace of her own hunger for a first chance to do an on-camera interview. She'd been fortunate, though. There were many people who'd helped her, including Richard Champion. Without their support she wouldn't be a news anchor today.

Had she paid their support forward and helped another wannabe reporter? The answer made her cringe. She couldn't recall one single person she'd helped. Instead of thanking God for all the blessings He'd showered on her, she'd spent years dwelling on the bad things that had happened in her life—her breakup with Alex, Richard's unfaithfulness and her father's attack. It was time for a change in her life.

Some things like her misguided infatuation with Richard and her father's injuries couldn't be changed, and she and Alex might never recapture their childhood friendship, but she could still be happy. She could start right now by helping a young reporter get her first story.

She smiled at Julie. "I think Derek had a good

idea, Julie. Let's do an interview that will get you noticed."

Julie glanced at Derek, and the look that passed between them reminded her of the way she and Alex used to look at each other. Out of the corner of her eye she saw Alex watching them also. A smile crooked his mouth, and tears filled her eyes. It was the same way he'd smiled at her when they were children and he approved of something she'd done. But they weren't children anymore.

She took a deep breath and motioned for Derek and Julie to follow her into the house.

Alex stood inside the Kincaids' den near the door and watched Julie discussing the upcoming interview with Grace. He remembered the day he'd gone to the TV station and how Grace had complained about the girl's incompetence. Minutes ago she'd agreed to let Julie interview her on a live feed.

He smiled and let his gaze travel over Grace who had always held everyone, herself included, to the highest standards when reporting the news. Why would she allow an unproven reporter to interview her on a breaking story? The answer came to him almost before the question had flashed in his mind. It was because of the path Grace's life had taken in her new relationship with God. Like her parents, her eyes had been opened to the needs in others, and she was different in many ways than she'd been before. He couldn't deny he liked the new Grace much better than the one he'd known all his life.

In an effort to bring his thoughts back to the matter at hand, he turned his attention to Julie who was bustling about the room like a director getting ready to stage a play. Her commanding professional attitude indicated she hadn't wasted her time at the station. She'd been watching, and she'd been learning. He hoped she could please Grace, who at the moment appeared to be following Julie's instructions to stand in the middle of the broken ornaments littering the floor from the fallen Christmas tree.

Julie turned to Derek for their last sound check. When they'd finished, he held up three fingers and mouthed the countdown to her. Julie looked into the camera with a no-nonsense expression on her face.

"This is Julie Colter coming to you live from the home of WKIZ news anchor Grace Kincaid. As much as I wish this was a social visit, I'm here tonight with Grace to discuss the vandalism of her beautiful home." She paused as the camera swept the room. "As you can see, some unknown person or persons entered the home while the family was away and left a trail of destruction throughout the entire house. Police are on the scene as we speak, and one of my sources tells me evidence has been recovered that may lead to an arrest." She paused and faced Grace. "This must have been a terrible shock when you arrived home tonight. What was your reaction when you walked in to find your home had been invaded?"

Alex couldn't take his eyes off Grace as she proceeded to relate the shock of walking in to find nearly everything in the house destroyed. With sympathy flickering in her eyes, Julie hung on every word Grace spoke.

Grace paused and then addressed the camera. "I'm sure anyone who has come home to find their home burglarized knows how violated I'm feeling right now. We read about these things happening or we see it on the news, but somehow we never think we'll be the victim of a crime. Yet it happens all the time."

Julie nodded. "You're right. According to statistics, a burglary happens every fourteen seconds, and the number is rising every year. We all are potential victims." She turned back to Grace. "One of the deterrents to home invasion is a security system. Does your home have one?"

"Yes, but unfortunately it wasn't working. Either my parents forgot to turn it on when they left or the burglar disabled it. If my parents did forget, we'll have to make sure they don't again."

"And speaking of your parents," Julie continued, "I know they aren't here right now. How are they holding up? Your father especially. We were all saddened when he was gunned down in a drive-by shooting earlier this year."

"They're doing all right. My father is strong, and he'll get through this. Whoever shot him may have taken the use of his legs away, but it's made a stronger man out of him. I'm very proud of him."

"That's good to hear. Grace, we only have a minute left, and I understand you'd like to make a statement to our viewers."

Grace smiled. "I would. As many of you know, a few days ago I reported the death of Timothy Mitchell, who jumped from the Memphis-Arkansas Bridge. He was the father of one of my high school friends who was thought to have committed suicide twelve years ago. Thanks to the help of Detective Alex Crowne, I have been able to investigate Mr. Mitchell's belief that his son was murdered. Our findings suggest he may have been right. In pursuing this case, however,

I've been shot at, poisoned by a cyanide-laced note and now my home has been vandalized."

"Excuse me, Grace," Julie interrupted. "Are you saying you believe Landon Mitchell was indeed murdered and his killer is responsible for the acts of violence you've suffered since you broke the story of his father's plunge from the Memphis-Arkansas Bridge?"

"I am. In fact, I'm convinced of it." Grace glanced over at him, and Alex smiled. Then she continued. "So, I want to take this opportunity to let the murderer, who thinks he can intimidate me, know his attempts to stop the search for the truth haven't worked. The police are on this case and before too long I expect they'll have the answer to who murdered Landon Mitchell and at least four other people. You can't stay hidden forever."

Julie frowned and leaned closer to Grace. "Those are brave words, Grace, and I'm sure our viewers wish you well in your search. Is there anything the public can do to help?"

"Yes, there is." She paused and took a breath. "One of you viewing this report may have information about the deaths of Landon Mitchell or Sam Jefferson, or about a secret high school club whose members were tattooed with a wolf. If you do, get in touch with me. You can leave a message on my voice mail at the station or you can email me at my address on the station's website."

Julie turned and looked at Derek as he zoomed in on her for a close-up. "Grace needs your help. If you have information, get in touch with her. In the meantime, keep watching this station for the latest developments in the investigation. This is Julie Colter for WKIZ news, live at the home of Grace Kincaid."

Derek signaled that the camera was off, and Julie let out a long breath. Grace smiled and patted her on the back. "Great job, Julie. I think you're right. Your talents are wasted working as a glorified gopher. When I come back to work, I'll talk to the manager about making you my assistant. Would you like that?"

Julie's eyes grew wide. "Oh, Miss Kincaid, it would be like a dream come true."

"Then that's what I'll do. Now I think I'd better check with Detective Crowne and see if I need to stay here any longer."

Derek nodded and grasped Julie's arm. "We'll get out of your way, Grace. I hope to see you back at work soon."

"I'll be back after Christmas."

Alex straightened from leaning against the wall as Grace walked toward him and smiled.

"Good job on the interview. If our guy saw it, he's probably trying to decide what he can do next to make our lives miserable." He let his gaze drift over her face. "I don't want anything to happen to you."

"I don't either, but we can't let him control us much longer." She propped her hands on hips and glanced around the room. "Do you think Clay could have had time to drive from Nashville and do this?"

"I don't know, but I doubt it. He looked more scared than angry, but that doesn't mean he couldn't be involved. He could have made a quick telephone call and set this in motion." He sighed and rubbed his hand over his eyes. "Every way I turn with this case new questions pop up, and I have this thought niggling in my head that I've forgotten something."

"But you can't figure out what it is?"

He shook his head. "It's like it's just out of reach of my memory, and I know it's something important. I'm missing something, but I don't know what."

She yawned. "Don't worry. You'll remember."

"I hope so." He sighed and glanced over his shoulder. "There's no need for us to stay here any longer. The officers can take it from here. Let's get you down to the Peabody, and then I'll go home and get some sleep. Maybe tomorrow will bring some new leads in the case."

"I sure hope so. I'll get my bag and be back in a minute."

He stood still and watched as she left the room. It had been a long day, and he was ready to get some rest. He hoped he could sleep. If only he could get this thought out of his mind that he knew something that could bring this case to a close right now. It was something someone had said. Not recently, but a long time ago. Something he should have remembered. But what was it?

After a minute, he exhaled and shook his head. There was no use racking his brain tonight. Maybe tomorrow he could remember what he needed to know.

ELEVEN

Grace swallowed the last bite of her omelet and picked up her coffee cup. Breakfast had always been one of her favorite meals, and nothing could be better than being served in the dining room of the Peabody Hotel. Her parents were having a quiet morning with room service, but she'd wanted to mingle with other guests and enjoy the beautiful Christmas decorations that had turned the hotel into a wonderland.

She'd attended many private parties at the Peabody and had dined here several times with friends, but this was the first time she'd ever spent the night in the elegant hotel. The visit would have been very exciting if it weren't for the reason she and her parents had become guests. Her forehead wrinkled as she recalled the events of the night before. When she'd checked on her parents earlier, her father had mentioned they needed to contact their insurance company, and she needed to take care of that right away.

She pulled her cell phone from her purse and was about to dial the number when she looked up and spied Alex walking in the door. Her pulse quickened at the sight of him. She'd always thought him handsome, but somehow this morning his presence set her heart to beating faster.

He stopped at the table and dropped into the chair across from her. "Sorry to be so late. I took advantage of it being Saturday. Since I didn't have to go to work, I slept in longer than usual."

"Do you want something to eat?"

He shook his head. "I ate before I left home, but I could use some coffee."

As if she'd heard the request, a waitress stopped beside the table. "Coffee, sir?"

He smiled. "Yes, please."

Grace waited until the woman had poured the coffee before she leaned closer. "How's the case you're helping Seth with coming along?"

"We're at a standstill, but it's a case that goes back a lot further that Landon's. We may never get the answer to that one."

Grace closed her eyes and shuddered. "It's horrible for families not to have answers. I hope we can find some about all the deaths of our classmates."

"Me, too." He looked down at the cell phone she still held. "Have you checked to see if anyone left you an email or a voice mail?"

"No, I was about to call the insurance company, but I think I'll check voice mail first."

Grace punched in the number and drummed her fingers on the table as she listened to the messages. From time to time she knit her eyebrows and shook her head. Every crazy in Memphis must have left a message for her, and they all claimed to know the killer's name.

She was about to give up when she clasped the phone tighter and sat up in her chair. "Hello, Grace, this is Sharon Warren," a woman's voice said. "I was Sharon Ashley when we attended school together, and I married Billy Warren. I'm in Memphis visiting my family for Christmas, and I saw your interview on television last night. I think we need to get together. I know some things that might help you with your case. You can reach me at 555-2721."

Alex set his cup down and frowned. "What is it?"

"I had a message from Billy Warren's widow. She wants to meet with me. She says she knows something that may help the case."

An excited look flashed on Alex's face. "When?"

"I have to call her." Grace punched in the number and waited for someone to answer.

A woman's voice answered. "Hello."

"This is Grace Kincaid calling for Sharon Warren."

"Grace, this is Sharon. Thank you for returning my call."

"No, it's I who need to thank you. I'm very much interested in talking with you. When can we meet?"

Sharon hesitated a moment. "I'm at my parents' home, and we're leaving to take my daughter to Disneyworld this afternoon. It's her Christmas present. Would it be possible for us to meet now?"

"Yes, I can do that. Tell me where."

"Why don't you come here? My parents have taken my daughter to the mall to get some last-minute items for the trip and won't be back for a while."

"We can do that." She pulled the phone away from her ear and whispered to Alex. "Do you have time to meet with Sharon?" He nodded, and she spoke into the phone. "Alex Crowne with the Memphis Police will be with me. It's been a long time since I was at your parents' home. What's the address?"

Alex pulled a pen and a small notepad from

his shirt pocket and slid them across the table to her. Grace mouthed a thank-you and wrote down the address as Sharon recited it to her. "And one more thing, Grace," Sharon said, "don't tell anyone else I'm in town. I still don't feel safe when I come back to Memphis."

"Okay. We'll keep this to ourselves, and we'll leave right now. We should be there in about thirty minutes."

"I'll see you then."

Grace ended the call and placed the phone in her purse. "Sharon doesn't want anyone to know she's in town. She sounded scared. Maybe this is the tip we've been looking for."

"I hope so."

Thirty minutes later they pulled to a stop in front of the address Sharon had given her. Grace stared at the rambling house with the circle driveway and remembered high school parties she'd attended here. "I haven't been to this house since we graduated."

Alex turned off the ignition and opened the car door. "I didn't know you and Sharon were friends."

Grace climbed out and looked over the car's roof at him. "We weren't close friends. Our families were members at the same country club, and I was always invited to Sharon's parties.

It's strange, though, I hadn't even thought of her since I heard Billy was dead. I don't know why I didn't."

Alex rubbed his neck and frowned. "I know what you mean. I've still got this feeling that I've forgotten something."

Grace walked around the car, and they climbed the steps to the front porch. "I'm sure it will come to you."

Before they could ring the bell, Sharon opened the door. Even though Grace hadn't seen her in years, she still recognized the girl she'd known growing up. She had matured, and her once-blond hair was darker than Grace remembered. But the blue eyes still crinkled at the corners when she smiled.

She reached out and grabbed Grace's hand in both of hers. "Grace, it's so good to see you."

Then she turned to Alex and shook his hand. "And Alex Crowne. You're still as good-looking as ever. Come in."

Alex's face flushed, and he grinned. "Thanks, Sharon. I didn't know if you'd remember me or not."

"Of course I remember you. Who could forget the guy who helped us win the state football championship?"

Alex's smile grew larger. "That was a long time ago."

Sharon rolled her eyes. "Don't remind me." She held the door for them to enter the house and led them to a study in the rear of the residence. When they entered the room, she closed the door. "I thought we'd talk in here since this is more private. Some of the household staff might pop into an open room while we're talking, but they won't open a closed door."

Grace sat down on a sofa and waited for Alex and Sharon to take their seats before she shifted to the edge of the cushions. "I was excited to hear from you. What is it you think might help us?"

Sharon took a deep breath. "As you know, Billy and I dated through high school. Everything went well until about midway through our junior year. Something happened to change Billy. He became surly, his grades dropped and he cut school all the time. I was so concerned I went to his parents."

"Had they noticed the change in him?" Alex asked.

"Yes, but they had no idea what was going on. Then when Landon died, it got worse. Billy became paranoid and said he was going to be the next to die. His parents were afraid he'd commit suicide, too, so they placed him in an institution."

A gasp escaped Grace's throat. "I'd forgotten Billy wasn't there to walk through graduation with us."

"No, he was off in another state undergoing treatment for a mental collapse. In the fall I started college at Rhodes here in Memphis, but I loved Billy, and I went with his parents to see him often. It was two years before he was able to leave the facility, but he said he couldn't live in Memphis anymore. His father had a business out in Colorado, so he gave Billy a job there. By the time I finished college, he seemed like the old Billy, and we were married."

Grace counted up the years in her head. "So you must have been married about four years before he died."

Sharon nodded. "I found out after we were married he wasn't the old Billy. He hardly slept at night. When he did, he'd wake up shouting all kinds of things."

Alex frowned. "What would he say?"

"He'd say things like 'I'm next' or 'Don't kill me.'"

Alex leaned forward. "Did you ask him about this?"

"I did over and over. Finally, one night he

broke down and told me that during our junior year in high school, he and Landon, Clay, Jeremy, Sam and Dustin had gotten some fake IDs and gone to a club in one of the seamier sides of the city. They were looking for some excitement in their lives, and they found it. Billy said the guys who hung out there were like characters you'd see in a gangster movie, but they were real. Billy and his friends wanted to be a part of that macho lifestyle, and before long they were pedaling drugs for their new friends. They made a lot of money selling to kids at school, and then they branched out with college kids."

Grace's mouth gaped open, and she turned to stare at Alex. "They were drug dealers. That explains the money Mr. Mitchell found in Landon's room."

Sharon nodded. "Things were going great for them. They were making money, hanging out with drug lords and thinking of themselves as smarter than the cops who were trying to get drugs off the streets. Then they began to get email messages from someone who warned them not to sell drugs to this one guy. Of course they ignored them. They thought they were untouchable. One day Landon emailed the others to tell them he'd found out who was sending the messages. He said he'd let them know that night. Instead, his car was found on the bridge."

"So he never told them who it was?"

"No, but the messages continued. The person who sent the messages said he had killed Landon, and each one of them would meet the same fate if they sold this man's son any more drugs. They wanted to go to the police, but they were scared. The last thing they wanted was for their parents to find out what they'd done. So they told their suppliers they were through selling, which didn't sit well with them. For weeks they were afraid they were going to die in a drive-by shooting, but the emails stopped."

"What happened next?" Alex asked.

"Billy had his breakdown and entered the hospital, and the others got their parents to send them somewhere for the summer before college in the fall. Dustin went to the Gulf Coast where he disappeared. By the time school started, the police had busted the drug ring, and their suppliers were in jail. They thought they were safe… that is until the letters began to arrive a year or so later."

Grace leaned forward. "What did they say this time?"

"They said the boy they'd been warned about selling drugs to had died of an overdose, and it was their fault because they'd gotten him hooked. They were warned to watch their backs because the Wolf Pack was about to pay for what they did."

"Wolf Pack?" Grace and Alex spoke at the same time.

"That's what the boys called themselves. They had a wolf's head tattooed on their shoulders."

Alex stared at Sharon. "Why didn't you go to the police with this?"

"Because Billy made me promise not to. He said if anything happened to him, I was to keep quiet. He didn't want me or our daughter harmed. A week later he died when his Jeep crashed through a guardrail and ended up at the bottom of a Colorado ravine. The police suspected his brakes might have been tampered with, but they couldn't prove it. I was scared, and I kept quiet." Tears sparkled in her eyes. "But when I saw Grace on television last night, I knew I had to come forward. This killer has to pay for what he's done."

Grace reached over and grasped Sharon's hand. "I'm glad you called. What you've told us lets us know that Landon was indeed murdered, and it looks like the others were, too. Did Billy tell you the name of the boy who died?"

She shook her head and wiped at her eye. "No."

"Did he mention anything that might give us a lead about where to start looking for someone who'd want to avenge his death?"

"No, he didn't…" She paused, and her eyes grew large. "He did say the guy was a college student, but they weren't the ones who sold him his first drugs. He'd started using when he was in high school. He mentioned that the first time they sold this guy drugs he was stoned out of his head and sitting on a motorcycle in a parking lot. Sam had been trying to get his dad to buy him one like it, and he kept asking questions about the bike. The guy mumbled something about it not being his but his father's."

"Is there anything else you can tell us?" Alex asked.

She shook her head. "I can't think of anything else."

Alex let out a big breath and rose. "You've been very helpful, Sharon. I hope you and your family have a great time at Disneyworld. Maybe by the time you get back, we'll have all this sorted out."

She stood and looked from one to the other. "I know Billy did some bad things, but he was really sorry about it later. It robbed him of his life, and our daughter will never know her father."

Grace hugged her and smiled. "Thank you,

Sharon. If we catch this guy, it will be because of your help."

She gave a small shake of her head and led them back through the house. "If I had done it earlier, Sam might still be alive."

When they were back in the car, Grace swiveled in her seat and faced Alex. "Are you thinking what I'm thinking? Mr. Donner rides a motorcycle."

He nodded. "That he gave to his son. But there are still some unanswered questions. I'm going to the station to search the police records for all the deaths by drug overdoses in the years following our high school graduation. When I get the names, I'll check each one out."

"But even if you have all the names, how will you be able to tell which one is connected to the boys from our school?"

"We know the kid who died was in college, so I'll pull out the ones that fit the age. Then I'll trace the families and talk with each one of them."

"That may take a long time."

He smiled and turned the ignition. "This is the way cases are solved, Grace. We follow up one lead at a time, no matter where it takes us. Sometimes it leads nowhere, and other times we find answers. There's still something I'm missing, and I'm not going to rest until I find out what it is. I'll take you back to the hotel first."

"All right. I told Mom I'd go shopping with her to buy replacement presents for the ones destroyed last night. We also have an appointment to stop by our decorator's office to discuss getting the house cleaned out and buying new furniture."

"What's your Dad going to do?"

"He'll stay at the hotel."

"Alone? What if he needs something?"

"That concerns me, too, but he assured Mom this morning he'd be all right."

"What if…" Alex hesitated as if he wasn't sure what he was going to say. "What if I stayed with him?"

Her mouth dropped open, and she stared at him. "You'd stay with my father? What about going to your office to check those records?"

He waved his hand in dismissal. "I can go later after you and your mother get back."

"No, I couldn't ask you to do that," Grace protested.

"Really I don't mind. I'd feel better knowing he wasn't alone."

Grace could hardly believe Alex had volunteered to stay with her father, especially with the history between the two. She blinked back tears and squeezed Alex's arm. "Thank you. It means so much to me that you'd offer to stay. Even though it looks like the suite may be home for us for a while, he still hasn't learned to navigate well in his new surroundings."

Alex glanced down at her hand on his arm and cleared his throat. "No problem. I'm glad to do it." He pulled free of her and reached for his seat belt. "So is your family planning to spend Christmas there?"

She sighed and buckled her seat belt. "It's not about the house where you spend Christmas, Alex. It's about being with the people you love. By the way, that reminds me. When will your father arrive for the holidays?"

"He's not coming. I talked with him this morning, and he's not feeling well. I'll probably leave Christmas Eve and drive down there."

"That's only a few days away. Will you be back for New Year's?"

"I don't think so. I've already put in for some vacation time. I'll probably stay a few weeks."

She hoped her face didn't convey the disappointment she felt knowing Alex would be gone all through the holidays. But if he decided to stay in Florida, he'd be gone for good. She forced a smile to her lips. "I know your father will be glad to see you."

He nodded and put the car in gear. He didn't speak as they drove back to the hotel, but Grace glanced at him every once in a while. The muscle in his jaw twitched, and she knew he was deep in thought. Whether it was about the killer they were after or his sudden decision to drive to Florida, she didn't know. Whatever it was, she wondered how much longer Alex would be in Memphis.

Alex still found it hard to believe he could feel so relaxed with Grace's father, the man he had feared most of his life. Now as he sat in the hotel suite and chatted with Harrison Kincaid he saw nothing in his demeanor that even resembled the arrogant bank president of a few years ago.

Mr. Kincaid took a sip of his coffee and set the cup and saucer on the tray of his wheelchair. "Thanks for sticking around to keep me company while Grace and her mother are shopping. They don't want the vandalism of our house to ruin our Christmas. I'm sure when they come back they'll have a tree as well as bags filled with all kinds of ornaments and presents to replace the ones damaged last night."

Alex smiled. "I was glad to stay." He let his gaze drift over the room. "This suite is very comfortable. Grace said you'll probably spend Christmas here at the hotel."

Mr. Kincaid nodded. "Of course we'd prefer to be in our home, but we're thankful we can be together. Why don't you join us for Christmas dinner? We'd love to have you with us."

"Thanks, but I'm going to Florida to see my dad."

"I'm sure he'll be glad to see you. Tell him I said hello."

"I'll do that. My father asks about you every time we talk. He always enjoyed taking care of the gardens at your house."

"He always did a good job. I hope you'll tell him I'm sorry for the way I acted about him bringing you along all the time."

"I'll tell him." Alex hesitated a moment. "About that…I still find it hard to believe how different you are now. I've heard people talk about how God can change your life, but I never saw it until now."

Mr. Kincaid nodded. "I suppose some people would think I should be angry because I'm unable to walk and confined to this wheelchair, but the truth is I'm happier than I've ever been. When I turned my life over to God, He filled me with peace and the greatest love I've ever known. If He can do it for me, He can do it for anybody." He pointed to his useless legs. "Don't misunderstand me, Alex. It's not easy, but I find myself able to cope with my disability because I trust God to make me content in my situation."

Alex's brow wrinkled, and he shifted to the edge of his seat. "But how can you trust something you can't see?"

"It comes from faith, Alex. It's a feeling inside that lets you know you're not alone, that you'll never be alone again. I have to admit some days I feel sorry for myself, then it's like a small voice whispers in my head and tells me I'm not alone. When I feel like I've gone as far as I can go, I turn it over to Him, and He gives me the strength to carry on. He can do it for you, too."

Alex shook his head. "I don't know."

Mr. Kincaid smiled. "Think about what I've said, and maybe we can talk about it again sometime. If you change your mind about going to Florida, then join us." He took a deep breath and pointed to a manila folder on his wheelchair tray. "Now if you don't mind, I have some work to do."

"I didn't realize you were still working," Alex said.

"I do a lot of work for the bank from home. These are some loan applications I want to study."

Alex chuckled. "I'm glad it's you and not me

making those decisions. It would be hard for me to turn down anybody for a loan."

Mr. Kincaid nodded. "It is. There have been people I knew and respected that I had to say no to because they couldn't afford to repay the money. I wouldn't have done them any favors if I had led them deeper into debt. Unfortunately they didn't always see it that way. I've had some really angry customers over the years." He glanced back down at the folder. "But that's all in the past. I think I'll go in the bedroom to work on these. There are soft drinks in the refrigerator. Help yourself and turn on the TV."

"I will, and I'll be right here if you need anything." Alex rose to his feet and watched Mr. Kincaid guide his wheelchair toward the bedroom. Just before he reached the bedroom door, Alex called out to him, "I enjoyed talking with you. I'll think about what you said."

Grace's father turned his chair around and smiled at Alex. "I hope you will." He swallowed, and his Adam's apple bobbed up and down. "I have many regrets, Alex, but my biggest one is that I interfered in your and Grace's relationship. If it wasn't for me, you two might be married, and I would be a grandfather. I don't know if I'll ever get that chance now. She'll never love anyone else the way she loved you."

"Mr. Kincaid, it wasn't..."

He held up his hand. "I know it wasn't entirely my fault, but I was determined to break you two up. Now I have no idea why. I didn't realize until I was shot how much I loved Grace's mother. I wasted a lot of years when we could have been happy." He paused and took a deep breath. "In spite of everything that's happened this past week, Grace has been happier than she has in years because you're back with her. She told me you might move to Florida, but I know she doesn't want that. I think you have to decide what you want. I've been praying you will discover what our family knows now—it's never too late for love."

Alex stood in stunned silence as Mr. Kincaid disappeared into the bedroom. He wanted to run into the room and tell Grace's father he wasn't to blame for their breakup. Alex could blame no one but himself. He and Grace could have worked out some sort of compromise if they had tried. Instead, he had declared that if she loved him, she'd give up her dreams, and she'd turned the same argument around on him.

It made him sad now to think how he had decided Grace was only concerned with her own needs and that he could never trust her to care about his. Then when she became engaged to

Richard Champion, he'd known he'd been right. Why hadn't he gone to her and insisted they work out their problems instead of letting years pass while resentment and anger build up in both of them?

For the past week they'd struggled to regain the trust they once had in each other, and they'd made progress. Even though she'd said she wanted his friendship, her father had hinted she still loved him. Was he ready to risk his heart again, or would it be best to walk away while he still could?

He sank down on the sofa and covered his face with his hands. He had no idea what to do.

TWELVE

Grace frowned and glanced at the clock on the bedside table. It was nearly eleven o'clock, and Alex hadn't phoned. When she and her mother had gotten back from shopping, he'd made his excuses and rushed off. She'd expected to hear from him by now to let her know if he'd found anything in the police records that might help solve their case.

Her parents had gone to bed early in the adjoining bedroom after dinner, and she'd rattled around the suite trying to entertain herself while she waited for a call from Alex. She picked up her cell phone for the third time to call him. Before she could punch in his number, she shook her head and laid it back on the table. He'd call when he had any information for her.

Thirty minutes later when he still hadn't called, she gave up and got ready for bed. She'd just gotten her gown and robe on when the phone rang. Her excitement over Alex finally calling died when a number she didn't recognize popped up on caller ID. She connected the call and raised the phone to her ear.

"Hello."

"Good evening, Grace. Did you have a good visit with Sharon Warren today?"

Her breath hitched in her throat, and she clutched the phone tighter. "H-how did you—"

"Know you saw Sharon?" her anonymous caller finished for her. "I know everything you've done for days. You'd think two people trained as a news investigator and a police officer would realize when they were being followed. You and Alex Crowne are pathetic."

She narrowed her eyes and gritted her teeth. "What do you want?"

"I want to tell you who killed Landon."

"And Sam, Dustin, Billy and Jeremy, too? You took care of the Wolf Pack, didn't you?"

A chuckle came over the phone, and a chill went up her spine. "So you think you know the whole story, but you haven't arrived at the full truth yet. Do you want to know?"

"Yes, what is it?"

"Don't be so eager, Grace. I'm not going to tell you over the phone, but I'm sure you're suspicious of meeting me."

Grace gave a snort of disgust. "I've tried

doing things your way. Once I was shot at, and the next time I was poisoned."

"There'll be nothing like that this time. I'm leaving town in a few minutes, but I've left you something."

"What is it?"

He sighed. "I'm tired, Grace. I've stalked the Wolf Pack for years, and I'm ready to finish my quest. In fact, I'm sitting on board a plane right now bound for Germany. I hope to meet up with Clay there. But don't get any ideas. We are taxiing to the runway and will be in the air before you can alert the police to my plan."

Grace sucked in her breath. "You won't get away with killing Clay. The police will notify the German police, and they'll stop you."

He laughed. "Maybe they will, but I doubt it. All kinds of accidents can happen on a ski trail. Afterward, I plan to disappear, and you'll never hear from me again. So I've left you something to remember me by."

"What is it?"

"I've made a video of my confession. When you see it, you'll know who I am and why I've done what I did."

"Where's this video?"

"It's in an appropriate place. I've left it underneath the entrance to the Memphis-Arkansas Bridge."

"Why there?"

He laughed again. "I thought since your interest in the Wolf Pack started on the bridge, it would be a good place for you to learn the truth. The video is easy to find. Leave your car at the E. H. Crump Park visitors' area and walk up the grassy rise toward the entrance to the bridge. At the top of the rise, walk down the slope toward the river, and you'll find the DVD in a box on the bank that runs underneath the bridge. Do you understand?"

"Yes, but how do I know I can trust you?"

"I suppose you'll have to decide. We're in line for takeoff right now, and I'm going to have to stow my cell phone. By the time you get to the bridge I should be safely away from the city. Goodbye, Grace."

Before she could say another word, the call disconnected. She stared at the phone, undecided what she should do. Alex would know. She punched in his number and waited as the phone rang. When it went to voice mail, she blurted out her message. "I just had a call from the killer. He's on a plane for Germany, and he's left me a recording of his confession. I'm going to find the video, Alex. If you get this message, meet me at the E. H. Crump Park near the entrance to the bridge."

She disconnected the call, tossed her phone on the table and ran to the closet. Within minutes she was dressed and ready to leave. She debated whether or not to leave a message for her parents but decided against it. She would be back before they woke.

Grabbing her purse, she hurried out the door and down to the parking garage where she'd left her mother's van earlier. She unlocked the car, jumped in and turned the ignition. She glanced at the menu panel on the dash and frowned when the Bluetooth didn't connect with her cell phone in her purse. With a groan she smacked the steering wheel with her hand. The phone wasn't in her purse. It was still lying in her hotel room. Why had she run out of the suite without picking up her phone?

Ignoring the urge to leave the phone behind, she leaned forward to turn off the ignition but froze when something round and cold touched the back of her neck. Only the barrel of a gun could feel like that. "Hello, Grace," a soft voice purred from the backseat. "I've been waiting."

She closed her eyes and berated herself. How could she have been so gullible? The answer popped into her head. She'd let the story become so personal that she'd lost her objectivity. She'd been quick to believe a killer, and now it might cost her dearly. "I thought you were on a plane."

"I lied."

Grace's heart thumped wildly, and she struggled to breathe. "Wh-what do you want?"

"I thought I'd ride with you to the bridge."

She clasped her hands in her lap and tried not to move. "How did you get inside this car?"

The sound of jingling keys echoed in her ear, and she cast a sideways glance at her mother's extra set of keys. "I found these when I was at your house last night. I must say they came in quite handy."

She straightened in her seat and lifted her chin. "So what do you have planned next for me?"

He gave a sharp gasp. "I want to tell you the truth. I thought we could all do it at the bridge. I'm sure you phoned Alex, and he'll be along shortly. Just the three of us at the bridge where it all started, but only one of us will walk away tonight. After you two are out of the way, your father will be next, then I'll get to Clay. That part wasn't a lie. I think he's about to have a skiing accident. As much as he drinks it won't come as a surprise to anyone."

He laughed when he'd finished speaking, and

the hatred in his voice made her skin prickle. "You're despicable. Why would you want to kill my father?" She almost spat the words at him.

"You'll find out in good time, Grace. Now drive. We don't want to keep Alex waiting."

She shook her head. "Not yet. Not until I know who you are."

"Then turn around and see."

She took a deep breath, looked over her shoulder and gasped at the familiar face smiling at her from the backseat.

Alex walked back into his office from his trip to the break room, opened the tab on the soft drink can he'd purchased and dropped down in his desk chair. He took a long drink and set the can aside before he turned his computer on and berated himself for not getting to the office earlier.

Grace and her mother had returned exactly when they said they would, and he'd begged off staying for dinner so he could go to his office. The truth was, however, he wanted to put some space between himself and Grace. After the conversation with her father, he felt the need to ponder everything that had happened in the past week.

So instead of going to his office, he'd driven

home, fixed something to eat and paced through his apartment for hours trying to decide what he wanted. Now at his office with the clock inching toward midnight, he was no closer to an answer than he'd been earlier.

He sighed, took one more sip from the soft drink and turned back to the computer. Looking through the records of several years for some unknown person might be a hopeless task, but he did have a few leads that might prove helpful.

He pulled a legal pad out of his desk and wrote Randal Donner at the top of the page. Underneath he began to write the things he knew about his former principal. (1) Rides motorcycles (2) Father of a son (3) Gave son his motorcycle and bought himself a bigger one (4) Denied drug use in school (5) Denied knowledge of a secret society.

Alex looked over the list, turned the page and started a new list under the heading Facts About The Killer. (1) Rides a motorcycle (2) Had a son who died of an overdose (3) Gave his son a motorcycle (4) Killed the boys who sold his son drugs.

When he'd finished, he laid both lists side by side. The two lists appeared very much alike. However, he didn't know if Mr. Donner's son had died, but he knew who would. He pulled his cell phone from his pocket and punched in Brad's number.

He answered after two rings. "Hello."

"Brad, it's Alex. I'm at the office working on something, and I wanted to run a few things past you."

"Alex, do you know what time it is? It's nearly midnight. What are you doing there so late?"

"It's this case about the kids at our high school. I feel like I'm so close, but there's something I'm missing. I thought I'd bounce some things off you."

Brad sighed. "Man, you need to get a life. You can't let work rule you. Take it from an old married man. You need a wife."

Alex snorted. "I'll think about that. In the meantime, I wanted to ask you about Mr. Donner."

"Our high school principal?"

"Yeah. What do you know about him?"

"Hmm, well, he's been at the school for years, and from what I hear, he's done a good job."

"Did you know he's in a motorcycle club?"

"Yes. It's a group of professional people who do charity rides for different organizations. They also do some mission work."

Alex's eyebrows arched. "What kind of mission work?"

"They go to motorcycle rallies and set up a tent where they speak to people about God's love. They've become well-known across the southeast for their work at events."

"Very interesting. And what about Mr. Donner's son?"

"Which one?"

"He has more than one?"

"There are three. The oldest is a doctor in Nashville, the middle one is a teacher at the University of Tennessee and the youngest one is in college."

Alex's phone beeped, and he pulled it away from his ear to stare at the screen. A message popped up that he had an incoming call from Grace. He'd return the call when he finished talking to Brad. He pulled the phone back to his ear.

"So, did Mr. Donner have a son who died?"

Brad was quiet for a moment before he answered. "No, I don't think so. Not unless he died in infancy. My parents have known his family for years, and they never mentioned a child dying."

"This son would have been college-aged."

"Then, no," Brad said. "I know he didn't have one die at that age."

Alex exhaled a long breath and drew a big X

through the page where he'd written the things he knew about Mr. Donner. "Well, that eliminates him as a suspect. My guy's son bought drugs from Landon and his friends, and he rode his dad's motorcycle. The son died of a drug overdose when he was college age. I guess I'll have to keep looking."

"Wait a minute, Alex. You say this guy's son died of a drug overdose?"

"Yes."

"Have you thought of Mr. Caldwell?"

Alex bolted upright in his seat. "What?"

"He had a son who died of an overdose. His body was found in an alley near the downtown area about two years after we graduated from high school. Don't you remember us talking about it? We were in college, and a guy we graduated with came by our table in the cafeteria and told us Mr. Caldwell's son had died of an overdose. He remarked how surprised he was because none of the students even knew he had a son. The boy had grown up with his mother in Chicago. Evidently he got into drugs, and she couldn't handle him anymore. So when he started college, she sent him to live with his dad."

Alex hit his palm on his desk and groaned. "I knew there was something I had forgotten. This is it. When Grace and I went to the school the other day, we talked to him, and he mentioned he had no family. Grace later told me she always felt sorry for him because he didn't have a wife and children. Thanks, Brad. You've given me the answers I needed."

"One more thing," Brad interrupted. "Mr. Caldwell also rides a motorcycle. In fact, he's in the club with Mr. Donner."

Alex clenched his fist and pulled it down in a victory salute. "Yes, this is what I needed. I need to find Mr. Caldwell's son's death record now. Maybe by Monday morning I'll have enough evidence to take it to the D.A. By the way, do you know his son's first name?"

"I think it was Dennis, but he went by Denny."

"Thanks, buddy. I owe you for this one. I'll see you Monday."

"See you then."

Alex disconnected the call and turned to the computer screen. Within minutes he'd found the death certificate of Dennis Caldwell. The death was ruled a drug overdose, and the next of kin listed the name Patrick Caldwell.

Alex sat back in his chair and smiled. Ever since he started in law enforcement, he had a deep desire to bring closure to a victim's family. Now with his job in the Cold Case Unit, he was able to do that. In Landon's case, however, it was too late for his father, but Grace would be happy.

At the thought of Grace, he remembered her call. He needed to let her know what had happened, but she might already be in bed. He picked up his phone and noticed she'd left a message when she called, maybe to tell him goodnight. Smiling, he retrieved the message, but his smile disappeared as he listened to what she was saying. His hand began to shake, and he groaned aloud.

"No!" he screamed when the message ended.

He willed his shaking fingers to punch in her number and waited for her to answer. When it went to voice mail, he yelled into the phone. "Grace, the killer is Patrick Caldwell. Do not trust him. I am on my way to the bridge. I hope you get this message."

When he'd hung up, he looked back at her message. It had been sent twenty minutes ago. The Peabody wasn't too far from the entrance to the bridge, and she had a head start on him.

Shoving the phone in his pocket, he ran from the building, jumped in his car and roared off to the park where Grace had told him to meet her. He hoped he wouldn't be too late.

THIRTEEN

Grace pulled the van to a stop in the parking lot where Mr. Caldwell had directed her. She then turned off the ignition and sat back in her seat. "What now?"

"Give me the keys," he said. She passed the key ring to him and locked gazes with him in the rearview mirror. He opened the back door, stepped out and motioned for her to do the same. When she stood on the ground beside him, he pointed toward the grassy rise that led to the side of the bridge. "Now walk up that way."

She turned around, and he stuck the gun in her back as they began their ascent toward the bridge. "You can't get away with this, you know. Alex will track you down and see that you go to jail."

"Don't waste your breath, Grace. Alex should have kept his nose out of this, and he would have been all right. Now he knows too much, so I have to get rid of him, too."

"How do you think you can escape? The police patrol this area all the time. Gunshots would bring them on the double. Then how are you going to get away?"

He chuckled. "I already have my escape plan. I stopped by here earlier and left my motorcycle underneath the bridge before I called for a cab to take me to the Peabody. I'll be out of here before anybody knows what's happened. Now get moving."

She walked a few more steps before she stopped and glanced over her shoulder. "But I don't understand. What is your connection to the Wolf Pack?"

"It's simple. They killed my son."

Her eyes grew wide. "You had a son?"

"Yes. His mother and I divorced before he was born, and she kept him in Chicago and away from me for years. When she finally sent him to me, he was a nineteen-year-old drug addict. I tried everything to help him, but it was no use."

"So your son was the one who died from the drug overdose?"

"Yes. I tried to keep an eye on him, but he hooked up with Landon and his friends right away. They were only too glad to sell him what he wanted."

"And you blame them for his death?"

"Partly, but I also blame the dealers in Chicago who got him started—there was someone else to blame, too."

"Who?"

"Your father. I could have saved my son if it hadn't been for him."

Grace's mouth dropped open, and she stared at him as if he'd lost his mind. "How on earth is my father involved in this?"

"When Denny got so bad, I knew he had to go into rehab, but I didn't have the money to put him where he'd get the best help. I went to your father at the bank and begged him." He hesitated, and his features dissolved into that of a madman. "I begged him," he yelled, "to give me a loan so I could put Denny in rehab. And do you know what your father did?"

"N-no."

"He turned me down without a second thought. I pleaded and told him it was a matter of life and death, but he called the guards in and had me removed from his office. When they were dragging me out of there, I told him he'd be sorry. And he was, when I put him in that wheelchair."

Grace's legs wobbled, and she struggled to stand. "You shot my father?"

He laughed. "Yes, and when I saw you on

television talking about Landon's father dying at the bridge, I knew I could hurt him even more if I killed you." He eased closer and grabbed her arm. "So you see this past week, it's been all about killing you." He put the gun to her head. "And that's what I'm about to do."

"Hold it right there, Caldwell. I have a gun pointed at your back." Alex's voice sent a shock wave of relief flowing through her. She'd known he would come. Before she could move, Mr. Caldwell grabbed her around the waist, whirled around, and held her in front of him with one arm while the other held the gun to her head.

"Hello, Alex. I wondered when you would get here. As you can see, we're at a standoff right now. You may shoot me, but you can't stop me from killing Grace. Now back off, or she's a dead woman."

Alex looked at her from perhaps ten feet away, and Grace held her breath. She sensed the hesitation in Alex, and she screamed at him. "Shoot him, Alex, before he kills us both."

Alex moved a step closer, his gun pointed at Mr. Caldwell. Suddenly, a police officer emerged from the darkness beside Alex, a gun in his hand. "What's going on here?"

Alex glanced over at him, but before he could

say anything two shots rang out. Alex and the officer both hit the ground.

"No," Grace screamed and struggled to free herself.

Mr. Caldwell's grip tightened, and he laughed. "I should have told Alex I've been trained in how to handle a gun."

A surge of energy rushed through her body, and she slipped one arm free from the vise he held her in. Raising her hand, she gouged at his eye and then dug her fingernails into the side of his face and pulled downward.

He screamed in pain, grabbed at his face, and released her. She drew her foot back and kicked him in the knee with all the force she could manage. He started to point the gun at her, and she kicked him in the other knee. He sank to the ground. "You'll pay for that," he yelled.

Grace longed to go to Alex and make sure he was alive, but there was no time for that now. In case he and the policeman were still alive, she needed to get Mr. Caldwell away from them before he finished the job.

She turned and ran toward the bridge and onto the walkway headed toward Arkansas. She'd only gone a few feet when she realized her mistake. She should be running back toward the streets of Memphis. There she could find hiding places and elude capture until she could get some help.

She turned to head back the way she'd come, and then she heard the engine of a motorcycle crank. Before she had time to process what that meant, the bike roared to life, and she heard it coming up the bank toward the bridge.

Mr. Caldwell stopped the motorcycle at the entry to the walkway and let the motor idle. He smiled and called out to her. "There's no escaping me, Grace."

The lights on the bridge lit the Memphis sky, and she realized she would be visible to any passing car. She glanced helplessly around, but there wasn't a single vehicle in sight. He revved the engine again, and she swallowed her fear. Slowly, the motorcycle glided onto the walkway and stopped. Breathing a prayer, Grace turned and ran toward the Arkansas side of the river.

Alex opened his eyes and saw the sky. The stars twinkled, and a peaceful feeling filled him. He blinked and tried to remember what had happened. The heavens appeared lit with a bright light, and he looked around to see where it came from. His gaze came to a stop on the lights outlining the bridge span between Memphis and Arkansas.

He tried to move, but a pain in his left shoulder ricocheted through his body. He gasped and grabbed at the spot where the pain seemed concentrated. A sticky substance covered his fingers. Blood. He shook his head to clear it, and the memory of Patrick Caldwell holding Grace in front of him and firing at him and another officer who had appeared out of nowhere flashed in his mind.

He pushed into a sitting position and closed his eyes to ward off the dizziness that had everything in his vision spinning out of control. After a moment his head cleared, and he opened his eyes and looked around. Where were Grace and Caldwell? From somewhere near the bridge an engine cranked, and a motorcycle roared out from underneath the abutment. He caught sight of Patrick Caldwell on the bike as it skidded across the dew-covered grass and sped up the embankment to the bridge walkway where it came to a stop.

Alex patted the grass with his right hand until he touched his gun. He picked it up and pushed to his feet. From somewhere in the darkness a woman's soft cries drifted on the night air. Grace? Where was she? On the walkway?

He pushed to his feet and clenched his teeth to keep from crying out at the pain in his shoulder. Patrick Caldwell's voice rang out from the top of the hill. "There's no escaping me, Grace."

Alex took a deep breath and willed his legs to move. With his left arm dangling at his side and his gun clutched in the other, he staggered up the hill. Perspiration popped out on his forehead even though the night air was cold. Halfway there he stumbled but regained his footing.

The engine revved again, and Alex staggered on. Grace must have gotten away from Caldwell, and he was the only one who could help her. Something warm trickled down his arm and dripped from his hand to the ground. He'd seen gunshot victims before, and he knew he was losing too much blood. His body screamed he didn't have the strength to go on.

Then words Grace's father had spoken welled up inside him as if he stood there on the banks of the Mississippi River with him. *When I feel like I've gone as far as I can go, I turn it over to Him, and He gives me the strength to carry on. He can do it for you, too, Alex.*

Alex looked up at the stars again. *God,* he prayed, *help me save Grace. She's the only woman I'll ever love.*

The motorcycle eased onto the walkway, and with renewed strength Alex charged up the embankment. He arrived at the end of the walkway just as Caldwell accelerated and headed down the concrete path. In the distance Alex saw Grace running in the opposite direction.

Taking a deep breath, Alex steadied his arm, aimed at the rear tire of the motorcycle and fired. The back tire of the motorcycle exploded in a blast that split the night air, and the bike skidded. Pieces of rubber flew into the air as the motorcycle crashed into one side of the walkway, veered across to the other side and hit the opposite wall. Caldwell struggled for control, but it was no use. The bike careened once more from side to side and jumped the barrier that separated the walkway from the highway.

The motorcycle landed on its side in the middle of the highway and skidded across the asphalt with Caldwell pinned underneath. Sparks like those from a Roman candle shot up from the pavement as the metal scraped the surface and the bike slid to a stop.

Alex climbed the barrier and stumbled across the road to where Caldwell lay unconscious. Behind him Grace's voice called out from somewhere down the walkway. "Alex, are you all right?"

She leaped over the barrier and reached him just as he sank to his knees. He laid his gun on the pavement, pulled his cell phone from his pocket and handed it to her. "Call 911. Tell them two officers and a suspect are down at the bridge. We need help right away. We have no way to stop traffic."

Grace nodded and grabbed the phone from his hand. He heard her speaking, but he couldn't concentrate on what she was saying. He slumped to the pavement and closed his eyes. All he wanted was to sleep, but he needed to stay awake until the EMTs arrived.

He licked his lips and swallowed. "Grace," he whispered.

She dropped to her knees beside him and grabbed his hand. "Help is on the way. Stay with me, Alex. Talk to me."

He stared up at her and tried to focus his eyes. "Are you all right?"

"I'm fine. Thanks to you."

"We're in the middle of the bridge. Watch for cars."

She clasped his hand tighter. "Don't worry about anything right now. I told the 911 operator. She's getting word to the Arkansas Highway Patrol to shut off that end of the bridge." She glanced past him and smiled as a siren wailed. "And here come our guys now."

A vehicle screeched to a stop near him, and then the sound of voices filled the quiet night.

Alex closed his eyes and thought of the mighty river flowing so far below them. The muddy water stopped for no one, and it felt as if he floated with it. He reached for Grace's hand and let the darkness carry him away.

Grace glanced at the clock on the wall as she paced the hospital waiting room. It was 3:00 a.m. Alex had gone into surgery two hours ago, and she hadn't heard a word.

The room and hallway looked like a constantly shifting sea of blue from the uniformed, on-duty police officers who arrived and then departed after checking on two of their own who had been shot. As Grace let her gaze travel over the assembled officers, she realized how fortunate Alex was to belong to such a brotherhood.

The sound of the elevator opening in the hall caught her attention, and she looked out the door to see Police Chief Watson striding toward them. Captain Wilson, the officer who'd been at the bridge the morning Mr. Mitchell died, rose from the sofa where he was sitting and met the chief at the door.

"Evening, sir," he said.

The chief nodded. "More like good morning, I'd say. How's Detective Crowne?"

"He's in surgery, sir. The bullet hit an artery,

and he lost a lot of blood. The EMTs said he was fortunate he got to a hospital so quickly."

"Good, good. And the other officer. How is he?"

"Patrolman Grayson suffered a head wound, but the doctors are optimistic. He's still in surgery, too."

"And the suspect? What's his condition?"

"Mr. Caldwell has a broken leg, a broken arm and multiple contusions. He's in surgery down on the orthopedic floor. I have officers waiting there for him to come out of surgery."

"Have the families been notified?"

Captain Wilson nodded. "Patrolman Grayson's parents are on their way from Nashville where they live. I've talked to Detective Crowne's father in Florida, but his friend Miss Grace Kincaid is here."

"It seems like you have everything under control, Captain. Good work." He turned and smiled at Grace. "I understand you and Detective Crowne have had an interesting night. Not only have you solved a twelve-year-old cold case, but you've captured the killer of four other people and the man who shot your father. Would you like to tell me about it?"

"I'd be happy to." Grace walked to a sofa, and the Chief followed. When they were seated, she related the events that began the year she and Alex were in high school and ended in the middle of the Memphis-Arkansas Bridge that night. When she finished, she clasped her hands in her lap and glanced toward the door. "Now I wish someone would come tell me how Alex is doing."

The elevator opened again, and Brad and Laura Austin rushed into the room. Grace ran to Laura and embraced her. "We came as soon as we heard. How's Alex?"

Grace pulled back from Laura and looked from one to the other. Their faces mirrored the fear in her heart. She'd held her feelings at bay ever since she'd arrived at the hospital, but with the arrival of her and Alex's two best friends her resolve flew out the window. She put one arm around Laura's waist and one around Brad's and dissolved into tears. They pulled her close and let her cry for several minutes before Brad pulled loose and led her to the couch.

She sank onto the hard cushions, and Laura sat down beside her. Brad stood in front of them. "Would you like something to eat or drink? Some coffee maybe?"

Grace shook her head. "No, thank you. I just want to know how Alex is." She looked from Brad to Laura. "I thought we were both going to die on that bridge tonight, and all I could think about was how we'd wasted so many years when we could have been happy." She burst out crying again.

Laura put her arm around Grace's shoulders and smiled. "It's not too late. You and Alex can still have a life together if you love each other."

Grace looked up, her vision blurred by her tears. "That's just it. I love him so much, but I have no idea how he feels about me. He still blames me for our breakup, and now he wants to move to Florida. What will I do if he leaves?"

Brad's eyes grew wide. "Move to Florida? He hasn't said anything to me about it."

Grace sniffed and wiped at her eyes. "Well, he has to me. He knows I love him, but it's like he wants to punish me and get as far away from me as he can."

Laura placed a hand on each of Grace's shoulders and looked into her eyes. "And just how does he know you love him? Have you told him so?"

"Well, no, but I've tried to show him with my actions."

Brad squatted down in front of Grace and smiled. "I think you and Alex have a communication problem. When you see him, tell him how you feel. Give him a chance to tell you his feelings. You and Alex have driven Laura and me crazy for years. We're ready for you two to decide if you belong together or not."

Laura laughed. "He's right, Grace. God has given you another chance with Alex. Don't ignore it because of what you think he feels. Find out."

Grace reached out and clasped Laura's hand, then Brad's. "I'm so thankful God gave me friends like you. I remember when you were going through all your problems, and look at you now. You're happy…"

"And we're going to have a baby," Laura interrupted.

"What?" Grace squealed. "Why haven't you told me?"

Laura smiled. "We just found out, and you've been busy the past few days."

Grace hugged her friend again. "Oh, I'm so happy for you and Brad. I knew you two were meant to be together."

"Just like you and Alex are," Laura said.

Before Grace could respond, she glanced up at the doctor walking into the room. She jumped to her feet, and all the police officers moved in to hear what he had to say. He approached Grace.

"Miss Kincaid, I believe you're the one who came in with the patient."

"Yes, doctor. How is he?"

"He's in recovery and doing well. He lost a lot of blood, but we were able to repair the damage. If all goes well, he should be able to leave the hospital in a few days."

A sigh of relief went up from the assembled officers, and they smiled and patted each other on the back. "We're all relieved to hear that, Doctor," Chief Watson said. "Detective Crowne is a valuable member of our force. Thank you for taking care of him."

The doctor nodded. "It was my pleasure." He turned to Grace. "The patient is awake and is asking to see you. Do you want to go in?"

"Oh, yes. I need to see him."

The doctor smiled. "I thought you might like that. Come with me. I'll take you back."

At the door Grace turned and smiled at Laura, who gave her a thumbs-up. She returned the gesture and followed the doctor down the hall. A few hours ago she had climbed over a barrier on the Memphis-Arkansas Bridge and feared Alex would die before she had a chance to tell him she loved him.

But he wasn't going to die. Not tonight. And God had given her this time to make things right between them. And that's what she intended to do.

FOURTEEN

Grace stopped at the entrance to the cubicle where Alex lay and took a deep breath. Her gaze scanned the tubes and machines hooked to his body, and her heart lurched. Had the doctor been honest with her about Alex's condition?

She spied a nurse coming down the hall and stopped her. "Excuse me. I wondered about all the tubes attached to Alex Crowne."

The nurse smiled. "That's standard after surgery. Don't worry. We'll probably disconnect some of them by the time he gets to his room."

Grace sighed in relief. "That makes me feel better. Is he awake?"

"He's been going in and out. You can have a seat in there and wait. The effects of the anesthetic should wear off soon."

"Thank you."

Grace stepped back into the room and walked to the bed. Alex's hand lay out from under the sheet, and she covered it with hers. She threaded her fingers between his and remembered how holding his hand had always made her feel so safe. She hoped he could feel the same from her now.

His eyelashes fluttered, and his eyes blinked open. He stared upward for a moment but then turned his head to face her. "Grace." Her name sounded almost like a croak coming from his lips.

She smiled and bent over him. "I'm here."

His gaze took in her face. "Are you all right?"

"I am because of you. I don't know how you were able to walk up to the bridge. I thought Mr. Caldwell had killed you." A tear rolled out of her eye, and Alex reached up with his free hand and wiped it away.

"I knew I had to get to you before he killed you."

She frowned. "But how could you walk? The EMTs were astonished that you could go that distance when you had lost so much blood."

"It was something your father said to me that got me there. He told me when he didn't think he could go any further, he asked God to take over, and He gave him the strength he needed. God did that for me, too."

She smiled and squeezed his hand tighter. "He'll be so glad to know that."

"Over the past week I've come to realize what a wonderful man your father is. I look forward to getting to know him even better."

Her eyes grew wide. "Oh, that reminds me. You don't know why Mr. Caldwell decided to add me to his list of victims."

He listened as she related what her old teacher had told her in the van. When she'd finished, he shook his head. "Your father told me there were people he'd been unable to approve loans for who hated him. I never thought any of them could be the murderer in our case."

Grace closed her eyes for a moment and shook her head. "It's just all so unbelievable, but we did it, Alex. We found out the truth about Landon's death just like we promised his father we would."

Her hand still covered his, and he tightened his grip as he glanced down at their intertwined fingers. "We did. Now what are you going to do with Landon's ring?"

She pulled free of him and held her hand up. The tiny birthstones in the ring sparkled, and she looked at it for a moment before she slipped it from her finger and dropped it in her purse. "This ring belongs in the past like so many things in my life do. I feel like I've helped an old friend by finding out the truth about his death, although I found out some things I was sorry to know. Now I can let that part of my life go."

"We did what we promised Mr. Mitchell. I wish he was here today to know about it," Alex whispered.

She took a deep breath and straightened her shoulders. "I do, too, but enough talk about sad things. We need to be happy. You're going to be all right, and there are some things about our past that we need to get settled."

"I think so, too, but first I have a question. Has anybody called my father?"

"Captain Wilson called him when he called Patrolman Grayson's parents. And by the way, that young patrolman is going to be okay, too."

"Good. So would you mind if I called my father before we talk about whatever it is you have on your mind? I want him to know I'm okay."

Grace nodded and reached for his cell phone, which lay on the bedside table. "Want me to connect it for you?"

He shook his head. "I have him on speed dial. I'll do it."

She handed him the phone and sat down in the chair beside his bed. He put the phone to his ear and waited for his father to answer. It only took a moment.

"Hi, Dad," he said. "I'm in recovery and wanted you to know I'm okay."

He nodded while he listened, and Grace gazed at his profile. Even with all the tubes and machines as well as a five o'clock shadow, she didn't think he'd ever looked so handsome. Her heart swelled with love for him. Now if only he could feel the same about her.

"Yeah, it looks like I won't be able to make it for Christmas."

Grace's heartbeat quickened. Maybe he wanted to spend it with her.

"I doubt if the doctor will want me to travel that soon," he continued. "I may have to postpone the trip for a few weeks, but I'm still coming."

Grace swallowed her disappointment. So his plans for going to Florida were still in place, which meant he still wanted the job there. She brushed at a tear in the corner of her eye.

"But when I come, I'm going to bring someone with me—my fiancée." He turned to look at her. "Do you think you can get some time off to go visit my father?"

All she could do was stare in dumbfounded disbelief and nod. Alex laughed and winked at her before he turned his attention back to his father. "Yeah, it's Grace. Who else would it be?

I'll call you later today and let you know how I'm feeling. Bye, Dad. I love you."

He ended the call and handed her the phone. "Dad said to tell you hi."

She frowned, shook her head, and placed his cell phone back on the table. Then she rose to her feet and stared at him. "What just happened here?"

"You mean the part about you being my fiancée?"

"Yes, where did that come from?"

He reached for her hand and laced their fingers together. "When I woke up on that riverbank and thought Patrick Caldwell was going to kill you, I regretted every minute that we'd been apart. I knew if God let us live, I was going to spend the rest of my life making it up to you for being such a jealous guy and ruining our chance at happiness years ago." He paused and pulled her closer. "I've never quit loving you, Grace. Please let me show you how much."

"B-but you told your father we were engaged, and you didn't even know if I love you or not."

"Yes, I do."

She smiled at him. "And how do you know?"

His eyes sparkled. "Because there's been a bond between us since we were ten years old. It grew deeper as we got older. I've never loved anybody else, and I never will. We've wasted enough years when we should have been together. If you'll marry me, I'll do everything in my power to make you happy. I'll leave Memphis if you want to go back to the networks. My life is meaningless if you're not in it. How about it, Grace? Will you spend the rest of your life with me?"

Tears filled her eyes. "I've loved you for as long as I can remember. I don't want anybody else but you." She leaned closer and squeezed his hand. "But I don't want the networks. I want to live our life together here where we met and grew up. All I want is you."

"Then marry me," he whispered. "I don't ever want to be away from you again."

"Neither do I. Yes, I'll marry you."

He released her hand, grasped the back of her neck and pulled her head down until their lips touched. "I love you, Grace Kincaid," he whispered.

"And I love you, Alex Crowne," she answered.

She pressed her lips to his, and her heart soared. The love they shared had never died, and she could hardly wait to begin their new life together.

Alex sat down on the sofa in the Kincaids' hotel suite, stretched his legs out in front of him and closed his eyes. He didn't know when he'd ever spent a better Christmas Day. The dinner prepared by the hotel staff had been delicious, but the best part of the meal had been Grace and her parents. The only thing that could have made it better would have been to have his father with them, but he would be here soon.

His father had decided that moving to Florida hadn't been the best choice for him. He'd missed the life he'd known in Memphis, but he'd especially missed being with his son. Now with Alex and Grace getting married, he wanted to be nearby in case there were grandchildren in his future.

The cushion next to him dipped, and he opened his eyes to see Grace sitting beside him. She had her arm on the back of the couch and one leg curled underneath her. She scooted closer and smiled. "What are you thinking about?"

"My dad. I'm glad he's moving back. With him nearby, I can keep a close watch on his health."

"We both will," Grace said as she leaned back into the cushions. "Did you get enough to eat?"

He groaned. "I'm stuffed more than the turkey was, but I think I'll be hungry again by nighttime." She laughed, reached over and trailed the tip of her forefinger down his jawline. He closed his eyes at the pleasure that raced through him. "I always liked it when you did that."

"And I always liked it, too." She leaned closer and brushed her lips across his. "It's almost been a perfect day, hasn't it?"

He nodded. "It has. Now all that's left to do is open the presents. I can hardly wait to see what you got me."

She laughed and arched her eyebrows. "If I'd had more time to shop, I could have gotten something better. But all my time these past few days has been spent playing nurse to a grumpy patient."

"And you've done a mighty good job, ma'am. I may decide to keep you around for quite a while."

She laughed and swatted his leg as the bedroom door opened and her father's wheelchair rolled into the room. Her mother followed behind. "It sounds like everybody in here has the Christmas spirit," Mr. Kincaid said as he came to a stop. "I move that we keep the festivities going by opening presents."

Grace clapped her hands and smiled. "And I second the motion. All in favor say aye."

All four yelled their response at the same time. Mr. Kincaid smiled at his daughter.

"Grace, do you want to do the honors and pass out the gifts?"

Fifteen minutes later Christmas paper and ribbons littered the floor. Grace jumped up and ran to give her parents each a kiss. "Thank you for everything you gave me. I love the clothes, and the jewelry will set each outfit off."

Alex held up his present. "Mr. Kincaid, I can't believe this. A private suite with catering and a server for the remainder of the Memphis Grizzlies' season? This is too much."

Mr. Kincaid waved his hand in dismissal. "Not at all. If you decide you like having the suite, I'll get one for the whole season next year. I do have to warn you, though, that Grace would rather go to a play at the Orpheum than see a basketball game. I thought if you didn't mind, I might go with you sometime."

Alex's throat closed up, and tears stung his eyes. He'd never thought to see the day when Grace's father would tolerate his presence, much less want to hang out with him at a ball game. It only reaffirmed what he was just beginning to understand—with God nothing was impossible.

"Thank you, sir. I'd like that a lot." He took a deep breath and rose to his feet. "Now there's something I'd like to do." He looked at Grace. "Please come sit down."

She looked at her mother and laughed. "This sounds interesting."

She sat down on the couch, and he turned to face her parents. "As you know, things happened rather quickly over the past two weeks. When I woke up in the hospital, all I could think about was how much I loved Grace and how much time we'd wasted being apart. When she came to see me in recovery, I'm afraid I didn't give her a very romantic proposal. In fact, I informed her we were getting married."

Her parents smiled, and her father shook his head. "That's all right. We're glad you're both safe and weren't hurt."

"I am, too, but I really feel like I should have talked with both of you before we started making plans. I really want to be a part of this family, and I want to make sure you want that, too."

Her father nodded. "You needn't worry, Alex. We couldn't be happier to have you for a son."

"Thank you, sir." He reached in his pocket with his good arm, pulled out a ring box, and knelt in front of Grace. He opened it and looked up at her. "Grace Kincaid, I love you with all my heart. Please marry me and make me the happiest man on earth."

Tears filled her eyes, and she looked at the ring, then back at him. "It's a beautiful ring.

And nothing would make me happier than to be your wife."

Smiling, he pulled the ring from the box and slipped it on her finger. "Now it's official. I don't want that ring to ever come off your finger."

"It won't," she whispered and leaned forward to kiss him.

They pulled apart, but Alex didn't want to move. It had been so long since he was this happy he wanted to keep looking at her and soak up every inch of the woman he'd loved since he was ten years old. After a moment her father's discreet cough caught his attention, and he rose.

"Have you two decided when you want to have the wedding?" her father asked.

Alex shook his head. "I don't know. We haven't had a chance to talk about where we're going to live. I don't think my apartment's big enough. Grace couldn't get all her clothes in the tiny closet."

Her mother laughed and nodded. "She'll need some room, that's for sure."

Grace frowned. "We also have to think about you two. Who will help you at night, Mother, if I'm not there?"

Her father shook his head. "You're not to worry about me. I'm going to hire a personal assistant as soon as we get back in the house.

We'll make it fine, and I don't want you to start married life with your parents. So I decided to do something about it."

Grace stared at her father. "What have you done?"

He picked up an envelope from the tray of his wheelchair and held it out. "This is for you and Alex with love from your mother and me."

Alex looked at Grace, and she shrugged. She took the envelope from her father, and Alex looked over her shoulder as she unfolded the papers inside. His eyes grew wide, and he shook his head in disbelief. "Mr. Kincaid, this is too much."

"No, it's not, Alex. You saved my daughter's life and helped bring the man who put me in this wheelchair to justice. I can never repay you for all you've done for me."

"But a house? You want to give us a house?"

Grace's father laughed. "It's only a starter house. You can sell it later on and move into a larger one when you decide to bless us with grandchildren. I spent a lot of years working for the money I accumulated. Now I want my family to enjoy it. The house belongs to you and Grace."

Tears ran down Grace's face. She ran to her parents and embraced them. "Thank you, Mom and Dad. I don't know what to say."

Her mother kissed her on the cheek. "Just be happy, darling. That's all we want for you."

"I will."

"Now," her father said, "if all the gifts are distributed, I think I'll take a nap." He looked at his wife. "Want to join me?"

She cast a glance at Grace and Alex. "I think these two might like to have some time alone."

When her parents had disappeared into the bedroom, Alex put his arms around Grace and pulled her to him. "I think your father had a good idea about leaving us alone. What would you like to do?"

Before she could answer, her cell phone rang. She pulled it from her pocket and smiled. "It's Derek from the station. I guess he's calling to wish us merry Christmas." She pressed the phone to her ear. "Hello, Derek. Are you having a good Christmas?"

She listened for a moment, and her smile grew larger. "Spending it with Julie? You don't say. It sounds like things are going well for you."

She walked to the window and looked out as she continued to listen. "That's the best news I've had in a long time. Thanks for calling to let me know. I'm looking forward to getting back to work, and tell Julie I'll be in touch in a few days. Bye, Derek."

She hung up but didn't turn away from the window right away. Alex frowned and took a step toward her. "Is everything okay?"

She looked over her shoulder and smiled. "This was already the best Christmas ever, but it just got a lot sweeter."

"How's that?"

"Derek called to tell me Todd has gotten a job as anchor at a Los Angeles television station. He's leaving after the first of the year."

He laughed. "So you got your wish."

She turned around and held out her hand. "But I got another one, too."

He walked to her and put his arm around her. "What's the second one?"

She pointed to the window. "Look outside, Alex. It's snowing. After all these years we finally got our wish for a white Christmas."

He looked out the window at the snowflakes drifting to the ground. Already a blanket of snow had covered the street. The memories of Christmases past and wishes made floated through his mind. He remembered the innocent children they'd been and the angry adults they'd become.

Outside the snow continued to fall as it covered everything and made a new world in the street below. That's what the love he and Grace had for each other was going to do. With God's help, their love would wipe away the hurts of the past and create a new life for them together.

Alex tightened his arm around her waist and pulled her close. She snuggled against him as they gazed out the window at the falling snow. Contentment like he'd never known welled up in him. Smiling, she turned to face him, and he brushed the hair away from her face and kissed the scar on her forehead from so many years ago. "I love you, Grace," he whispered. "This is the perfect ending for a perfect day."

* * * * *

Dear Reader,

I hope you enjoyed reading Alex and Grace's story. When I first began to write this book, it was hard to imagine how two people who'd been childhood friends could wind up as angry adults. Then I realized jealousy, anger and imagined betrayal can sever the tightest of bonds. As I wrote their perilous journey toward the truth, I wanted them to learn what I've known for many years—God's love can sustain us in our darkest hours. It is my prayer that if you haven't found the strength that comes with knowing God's love, you'll tune your heart to His voice. Then you'll know, like Alex and Grace, that He can fill you with peace and give your life new meaning. He's waiting to hear from you.

Sandra Robbins

Questions for Discussion

1. Alex and Grace were childhood friends but became alienated as adults. Has this ever happened to you and a friend?

2. Grace had difficulty getting along with her coanchor Todd at the television station. Have you ever had to deal with someone in the workforce you didn't trust?

3. As a child, Alex was intimidated by Grace's father. What does the Bible say about how adults should treat children?

4. Grace's father became disabled after being hurt in a drive-by shooting. Are you acquainted with anyone who deals with a disability? How do you minister to that person and their family?

5. When the Kincaids' house was vandalized, they didn't mourn their lost possessions. Instead, they thanked God their family hadn't been harmed. Are the things you own of the greatest importance to you? What is?

6. Alex and Grace's high school classmate Billy Warren suffered a mental collapse dur-

ing their senior year. Have you ever had to deal with mental illness in your family or with a friend? What presented the greatest challenges to you about the experience?

7. Sharon Warren possessed information that might have kept someone from being murdered if she had gone to the police. Do you believe witnesses who withhold information from the police should be punished? If so, how?

8. Grace's father asked Alex to forgive his past attitude toward him when he was growing up. Do you find it difficult to forgive those who have wronged you? What does the Bible say about forgiveness?

9. Although Julie Colter had made mistakes in her job at the television station, Grace was willing to help her prove her worth as a reporter. Did someone help you once by giving you a second chance? How have you paid that blessing forward?

10. Alex found perfect peace for his battered heart when he put his trust in God as Grace and her parents had done. Have you put your faith in God and accepted His gift of love?

LARGER-PRINT BOOKS!

GET 2 FREE
LARGER-PRINT NOVELS
PLUS 2 FREE
MYSTERY GIFTS

Love Inspired.
SUSPENSE
RIVETING INSPIRATIONAL ROMANCE

Larger-print novels are now available...

LISLPDIR13R

LARGER-PRINT BOOKS!

GET 2 FREE
LARGER-PRINT NOVELS
PLUS 2 FREE
MYSTERY GIFTS

Love Inspired

Larger-print novels are now available...

ReaderService.com

Manage your account online!

- Review your order history
- Manage your payments
- Update your address

> ### We've designed
> ### the Harlequin® Reader Service
> ### website just for you.

Enjoy all the features!

- Reader excerpts from any series
- Respond to mailings and special monthly offers
- Discover new series available to you
- Browse the Bonus Bucks catalog
- Share your feedback

Visit us at:

ReaderService.com